ALWAYS LIVING
THE DREAM

John Mihalyo

ISBN: 978-1-5356-1081-0

DEDICATION

To all my family and friends, who have provided me
with a plethora of memories and ideas, enabling me to
write this book. I love you all.

TABLE OF CONTENTS

ACKNOWLEDGMENT

A special thanks to Deb Z. who worked hours deciphering my handwritten documents and typing them into a legible manuscript. I am also grateful to Doctor Jack Hattman for his taking time to critic the book.

INTRODUCTION

Life is full of ups and downs. We all have good days and bad days. This said, we must all persevere to live our life to the fullest. In the Bible, Jeremiah, in the book of Jeremiah, Chapter 20, verses 10 through 12, felt as though he had his back to the wall with no place to go. He says, "Yes, I hear the whisperings of many: 'Terror on every side!' All those who were my friend are on the watch for any misstep of mine."

He keeps the faith by going on to say, "But the Lord is with me like a mighty champion. My persecutors will stumble, and they will not triumph."

We all feel we are in the same situation as Jeremiah at times. When this occurs, we must continue to live our lives to the fullest. We must look to our families and friends for support. We must keep our minds busy with something to do, have someone to love, have something to believe in, and something to look forward to.

There is nothing wrong with us having a dream, something to keep us going, especially when times get difficult. We all have good memories in our lives. When a bad day comes around, we should set our minds on the good times, fun times with our spouses and children, a special trip or meal that we had together.

They say it takes more muscles to frown than to smile. As you read this book, I hope you have a lot of smiles. Our days on this earth are few in relation to the years it has been here. We should all remember yesterday is history, tomorrow is a mystery, and today is the present, a gift. I hope you enjoy this book, my gift to you.

CHAPTER 1
THE MORNING

THE SUNLIGHT BEAMED THROUGH THE blinds in my bedroom. The bed was so comfortable, but I knew after rolling over a few times and hoping that my occasional lower backache would not flare up this day that it was time to open my eyes and get moving. Let's go, Jake Million, up and at 'em. As is my ritual every morning and evening, I give thanks to God with a prayer.

"Dear Lord, thank you for blessing me through the night, and allowing me to awaken to the day you have provided. I pray for forgiveness for my sins, and thank you for all the blessings you have bestowed on me and all my family and friends, both in heaven and on earth. I pray for your continued blessings on all of us this day that we all may grow stronger, mentally, physically, and spiritually, to better serve you. I thank you for your blessings and pray for your continued blessings this day, and all the days of my life. Amen."

After my morning prayer, I made my way to the bathroom to brush my teeth and wash. It was now coffee time. I have no problem with caffeine, but I have a problem without it. I proceeded to the kitchen to my one-cup coffee maker and pushed the power button. While waiting for the ready light, I added some water and selected my choice of coffee for the day. Today's choice was dark roast. I then moved to the refrigerator to get out the milk to add to my morning brew. There were still a few slices of lemon cake left, which goes great with whipped cream cheese.

The coffee was brewed, the milk added, cake and cream cheese prepared voila, breakfast. I thought about the words of Churchill: "I am a man of simple tastes usually satisfied by the best." This is as best as it gets this day for breakfast. This particular day happened to be Sunday, and after finishing my coffee and cake, it was time to make the bed, and then I head to the shower. My intention was to make it to the nine a.m. Mass at St. Blaise's Church. I had plenty of time. I dressed in a pair of gray slacks, a fresh starched white shirt, neatly shined black loafers and a blue blazer. I then proceeded to the garage where my Mercedes turned right over and I was on my way.

Since I was early, I decided to stop by Bessie's diner for a second cup of java before heading down to see Father Matthew at St. Blaise's. Bessie's had the usual crowd, guys stopping in for their morning coffee and or breakfast before heading in for the daylight shift at Follansville Steel. There were also a few that had just ended the midnight shift, and were stopping for breakfast before heading home to get some sleep.

Bessie Ross was the owner of the diner. The eatery establishment was not a fancy place, but the food was good and affordable. There was a counter with about ten stools, as well as about a dozen tables with chairs, and a few booths added to the total. I had known Bessie for years. She was a good friend of my mother, and was at our home occasionally for card club when I was younger. The relationship has continued through the years.

"Good morning, Bessie," I said.

She responded with "Good morning to you as well, Jake. What can I get you?"

"Nothing at the moment, Bessie. I'm going to take a quick walk down to Moose's to see how the weekly card game is going, and say hello to the boys. I will be back shortly for a cup of joe."

John Mihalyo

CHAPTER 2
THE GAME

SATURDAY NIGHT HAD LONG GIVEN way to Sunday morning, but the boys at Moose's place had not even noticed. They usually never did. Their mind was on one thing, and that was the cards being dealt across the table for their weekly Saturday night game – four or five diehard card players who you would think would rather play cards than eat. The players were usually the same, with an occasional new face if, through some wild circumstance, one of the stalwarts had to opt out for a night. They were so serious about the game, if they couldn't make it, they would call Moose so he could get a replacement. The games varied, but usually it was pinochle or some variation of gin rummy.

Moose Wayne was the man in charge. He owned the small cigar store that housed the back room where the game was played. The store was an old establishment that was entered off the Main Street sidewalk. As you entered, you walked on an antiquated tile floor, mostly original, that showed the wear and tear of years of mill workers coming in to buy their cigarettes, cigars, gum, and chew, all that was required to get them through a day's work in the plant. All transactions were done at a counter with glass in the front and top to show the goods available for purchase. The money was deposited in a cash register that was most likely there when Moose's father first opened the store shortly after the Great Depression. The numbers on the register keys were highly worn, but the vault served the purpose of holding the funds.

I entered the back room and greeted all at the table. It was as if I were not even there. This morning, like most Sunday mornings, the attention was on the cards, as the usual readers of the rectangles were all present.

First in line, of course, was Moose. It was his place and he reined over the game. He sat in his chosen place with his usual attire, a red flannel plaid shirt that hung out over his belted trousers and his trademark brown pork-pie hat that was well broken in. The front of the hat showed many years of finger stains where Moose continually adjusted and readjusted it as the hands were dealt and the plays were made. The other staple that the proprietor was almost always never without was his plastic-tipped small cigar, usually not lit. This was a vital part of his game uniform.

Things were silent, and Moose finally could not take it anymore and yelled out to Dick "Butch" Graysen, "If you shuffle those cards much more you're going to wear the marks off of them. Deal the damn cards."

Butch was a nervous type and would say and do things without realizing what he did. "Okay, Moose. I was not shuffling them that long."

Louie "The Greek" Kornflakis chimed in, in his very low, easy-going voice as he rubbed his thinning head of hair, "Yes, you were, Butch. I almost fell asleep waiting for the next hand to start."

The fourth player for the night, Anthony Aroni, whom they called "Mac," adjusted his trademark fedora then, while running his finger across his Boston Blackie moustache, he warned Butch, "One more shuffle and I am going to reach across the table and smack you right across the head."

Mac would do it. He had the reputation of being a pretty tough guy, never one to back down from a fight, as far back as anyone could remember, and he usually won.

"Go easy on the boy, Mac," Moose voiced. "The kid is like my ward. I have to look after him. He's learning."

"So boys," I asked with a slight grin, "who's winning the money this week?"

Moose looked out from under his hat. "The Greek. I thought it was the Irish that were supposed to have the luck, but Louie here has cleaned our clock."

I smiled at Moose's demeanor. The guys all wanted to win in the worst way, not for the money as much the bragging rights, but they were happy to take their opponents cash.

"Hey, you guys are busy. I'm heading back to Bessie's. Come on down if you like. I'll buy the coffee."

They all responded in their own manner.

"Yeah, sure."

"Thanks, Jake."

"See you later."

I knew their mind was on the game. I exited the door and headed back to Bessie's. The journey back to Bessie's required me to cross the main street. I looked both ways and thought the path to be clear, but just as I started to cross; a car came speeding out of a side street and nearly ran me over. It happened very quickly, and the near miss caused me to go down briefly. I returned to my feet, brushed myself off, and went into Bessie's. Bessie and a few of the customers heard the commotion, and she inquired as I entered, "Are you okay, Jake? We heard the car go speeding by. That was a close call."

I assured Bessie I was fine. I took my seat in the booth against the back wall. Business had slowed, and Bessie took a seat across from me in the booth.

"You sure you're okay, Jake?"

"Yes, I am great."

"Okaaay." As if she did not believe me. "So how's the unofficial mayor of Follansville?" Bessie asked.

"If you're referring to me," I responded, "I am always living the dream. Thanks for asking."

Bessie shot back, "Come on, Jake you're one of the most respected people in all of Follansville. You're polite to everyone, whether you know them or not. What do you always say – 'It does not cost anything to be nice to someone.' You look great, you stay in good shape. That swimming at the community center and staying away from those sweets you like so much have kept you looking fine. You sure do not look your sixty-plus years."

I blushed, but Bessie continued. "Your attire is always neat and clean. I know it is Sunday and you're going to Mass, but look at you, well-pressed trousers, starched clean shirt, shined shoes, and clean-shaven. The women are always commenting on how handsome you are, and I know a lot of them who would jump at the chance for a night on the town with you."

"Come on, Bessie," I said modestly.

"All right, let's talk about something else," Bessie suggested. "How's your golf game? You must be playing some, it has been a hot summer and you have kept a nice tan."

I replied that I had been playing a couple of times a week with "The Geritols." The Geritols were a group of over-sixty-five-year-old retirees. For those that remember, Geritol was a product that was supposed to help those getting up in age to have some energy, thus the group's name.

"It will not be long, Bessie, before I will be heading to my place in Florida for the winter. You know the cold weather is not my bag. Give me the sun, the beach, and the warm weather. I am thankful to God for allowing me to retire from Follansville Steel after nearly forty years. The pension I receive, plus Social Security and some fortunate investing, has allowed me the life I enjoy."

"You deserve it, Jake."

"Thanks, Bessie. And I appreciate all the things you have done for me over the years."

"I'm just looking out for you, Jake. I have been doing it since you were a kid. I have been around this town a lot longer than you. I knew your mother, Hilda. She was a fine lady, and she always said to me, "if I am gone and you're still here, keep an eye on my son." She was really proud of you. She always bragged about her firstborn. Of course she had a lot to brag about. You weighed over eleven pounds at birth. You were always brought in solo by the nurse because you were such a handful."

"Thanks again, Bessie. You're the best." I leaned over and kissed her on the cheek.

"So what will it be this morning?" Bessie asked.

"How about eggs over medium, home fries, bacon, rye toast, and coffee."

"You got it, honey," replied Bessie.

As I waited for my food, I heard a disagreement going on a few booths away. Two young guys were giving

Bessie a hard time. She could hold her ground pretty well, but these two would not let up.

"Come on, grandma, cook the food right. These are the worst pancakes I have ever tasted, and his eggs ain't much better," one of the two blurted.

As Bessie stepped away, I saw fit to get involved. I approached the booth occupied by the troublemakers.

"Is there a problem here, boys?

The two looked at me as if to say, "what's it to ya?"

"Who are you, pal, the kitchen police?" one commented.

"No. I am a friend of Bessie's, and when people show her disrespect, I have a problem with it."

"Oh, yeah? So what are you ..." and before the sentence could be finished, I took the plate of pancakes and smashed them in the one's face, and the eggs went in the face on the opposite side of the table. I yanked them both out of the booth by their collars and, after having them lay five dollars each on the table to cover the bill, I escorted them out the door, politely telling them not to come back until they learned how to show some respect.

As I went back inside, the few patrons that were there gave me accolades for what I had done. Bessie, being her usual tough self, looked at me, saying, "You did not have to do that. I've handled worse, but thanks."

"No problem," I responded. "Is my order ready? I have to eat and get over to see Father Matthew. I have to give thanks to God for all he has given me."

I give thanks every day at different times of the day. It's never a bad time to pray. I remember telling two young girls on the high school swim team to pray while they were training. What better thing to do. Swimming all of those laps gets monotonous. You might as well say your prayers. When I see them now that they're grown and graduated from college, they still remember what I suggested.

I finished my breakfast. As I was leaving, I voiced to Bessie, "Have to go, Bessie. See you later."

CHAPTER 3
THE PLANT

IT WAS A BEAUTIFUL MORNING so I decided to leave my car in Bessie's parking lot and walk to Saint Blaise's. There was hardly any traffic this hour of the morning on Sunday. The strip mill was one block over from Main Street, and back in the day, it was usually very noisy, but not any longer. I thought of my first days in Follansville Steel, as a summer employee while going to college. The mill had a local union and they had a lot to say on who was hired for summer work. Good workers' sons received preference. My dad, Big John, as he was known by his fellow workers, was a dedicated employee. This helped me obtain summer employment. You never said anything bad about Follansville Steel around Dad. He made this fact known on more than one occasion that, thanks to the mill, we had food on the table and clothes on our backs. I remember witnessing an occasion when my dad and another fellow got into a heated discussion. The other guy said the wrong thing to my dad about the plant, and he was sent flying across the room into the corner. Needless to say that ended that conversation.

I thought about my first summer after graduating high school. It was then that I received my first taste of the plant. My first assignment was in the sheet mill. This was the same department that Dad worked in for many years. I wondered that summer if I worked in a steel mill or a lumber yard. Four-by-fours were used to brace the coils, and once the steel was moved, they had to be removed and stacked, and the floor swept. I stacked plenty of them. I was just glad to have a job.

I thought of what the plant was like back then. Follansville Steel was a fully integrated mill. The plant facilities started with a coke plant, which supplied coke to the blast furnaces. The blast furnaces provided the iron to the open hearth to produce the steel. This facility was replaced by a basic oxygen process, or BOP, as it was referred to, that made the steel in a more efficient manner. The steel was then poured into ingot molds to be reheated and rolled at either the Blooming Mill or Slabbing Mill. As modernization took place, a continuous caster was added to make slabs directly from molten steel. This part of the plant, from coke plant through the BOP, was referred to as the primary area.

I remember seeing the red-hot steel slabs being sent to the hot strip mill via railroad car. They were unloaded and stored in the slab yard until they were scheduled to be run on the hot mill. The slabs were rolled into coils. These coils were shipped out for further processing, where they were either tin coated for use in soup or beverage cans, or zinc coated for use in the auto industry. Follansville Steel even made structural products, such as I-beams used in home building and warehouse construction. Employees were permitted to buy the beams, and many homes in Follansville have beams that were made at the plant.

Times have changed over the years, my thoughts continued. How depressing, a once-thriving mill with twelve thousand plus employees was mostly idle, except for a small segment of what once was. The number of employees was now less than a thousand. The once-thriving Follansville Steel had gone bankrupt, and was bought by a large world international steel producer, and what remains is to their discretion. I am thankful it survived as long as it did. A lot of families had food on the table and a roof over their heads for a lot of years thanks to Follansville Steel.

John Mihalyo

CHAPTER 4
THE SURPRISE

As I WALKED DOWN THE street, I seemed to be daydreaming a bit, thinking about the mill and how depressing it was to hear the quiet. Only a few blocks from Bessie's, there was an alleyway between the buildings. Upon passing the opening, a blur appeared to my side, and a punch followed, knocking me into the alley. I was now aware that "pancake face" and "egg wash" were out to retaliate. They followed up their sucker punch with additional blows that dazed me. I parried the blows as best I could and returned some punches of my own, but these jerks were out for blood, and mine was whose they wanted.

I backed myself against a large green dumpster so neither foe could get behind me. My heart was beating faster and my breathing was getting tougher.

"So you think you're smart, messing with us, huh, pop? You messed with the wrong people. We are going to whip your ass."

A punch knocked me to the ground and the thought quickly went through my head that I could be in for a big butt-kicking because of the surprise attack. Just as I thought all was lost, some new punches entered the fray.

Lefts and rights were applied to the attackers, as well as a two –by- four being cracked across their backs, arms, and legs. The cavalry had arrived, and not a minute too soon, as far as I was concerned. The two aggressors ran, and as I looked up from the ground, I heard, "Saved your tail again, huh, big boy? I've been looking after you since our college days, and I still have to."

There with a smirk on his face and a two-by-four in hand. It was Luke Turkal, my best friend and confidant.

"What took you so long?" I replied jokingly.

Luke, who preferred to be called "Turk," had saved me from what could have been some serious hurt. He helped me up and dusted me off a bit. The two friends and fraternity brothers, who were as close as real family blood, embraced.

"Thanks, bro," I said, "you know I love ya," while applying a hug.

Luke responded with an embrace of his own.

"So how did you happen to come by, and just in the nick of time, I might add?"

Luke responded, "I stopped by Bessie's for coffee. I must have just missed you. She told me you were heading to St. Blaise's for Mass, so I hustled down this way, thinking I might see you. When I saw the action in the alley, and saw what looked like you needing help, I pulled this two-by-four out of a pickup truck parked on the street, and thought it a good opportunity to display the swing that made me an all-state baseball player. How did I do?" Luke questioned.

"You have my vote, bro," I voiced.

Luke responded, "You okay? Did they do much damage?"

"No, I am good. I was able to get my sport coat off and was able to swing a little better. My shirt is soiled a bit, but no blood. Do you want to come to St. Blaise's with me?" I asked. "Mass is going to be starting soon. I have lots to be thankful for. So do you, right?"

"Yeah," said Luke, "like the time we hit the wall entering the bridge in Wheeling doing about eighty with ol' Joey Zarik in his 442 Oldsmobile. We definitely had a few too many that night."

I laughed, although it was not funny at the time. "I remember us getting out of that car and the officer saying how lucky we were that the car did not flip over the retaining wall and fall about fifty feet into oncoming traffic. When Joe told us what his plan was, to approach the bridge at a hundred miles an hour, I put on the seat belt. I never wore one before, but it saved me from going through the windshield that night. I know we went to Mass that morning."

Luke grinned. "Yeah, I remember that. We were lucky. But I am going to pass today, Jake. Say a prayer for me. I will do my worshiping at my church. Do you want me to escort you to St. Blaise's so you get there safely?" said Luke as he displayed the two-by-four he still held in his hand.

"No thanks, Luke. I am only a block away, and I think those guys are in no condition for more action after you initiated them with that piece of lumber. I'll give you a call later."

With that, two good friends parted ways. Luke headed home to Elm Street. I finished dusting myself off, put on my blazer, tucked the newspaper, the *Follansville Review* that I had purchased in Bessie's under my arm, and headed for St. Blaise's for Sunday Mass.

CHAPTER 5
THE SERVICE

I HAD ONLY A SHORT distance to walk to get to St. Blaise's Church. As I approached, I could see the cars parked in the church lot and some of the parishioners entering the building. There was still a little time before Mass was to start, and I noticed Father Matthew Dean outside the door welcoming the congregation. Father Matthew Dean was a great asset to St. Blaise's. He was very well liked and respected by the entire parish. He was in his fifties, of average height with a very muscular weightlifter's build. Everyone always wondered how Father Dean kept up the pace of his daily routine. He was up at five thirty a.m., and off to the gym by six. The gym was near the rectory where he lived, so he walked over and back every day. By seven thirty, he was back to offer morning Mass each weekday. On Sundays, he would offer four Masses at eight, ten, noon, and five in the evening. When he was not offering Masses, he would take care of any other pastoral duties required of him, as well as satisfactorily overseeing a grade school and high school. He was in great physical and mental shape. He needed to be.

As I approached, Father Matthew recognized me and greeted me warmly. "Good morning, Jake, how are you doing?"

I replied, "Always living the dream, Father. How about you?"

"Jake, I am so good; Webster has not come up with a word to describe it."

"You're the best, Father. I hope the bishop knows what he has in you. Everybody at St. Blaise's knows."

"Thanks, Jake, that's very kind of you to say. Listen, Jake, I have to get ready for Mass, but I would like to talk with you a little more. How about staying around after Mass?"

"Sure, Father, I'll do that."

I took my place in one of the pews, being careful not to sit in a seat that was normally occupied by a member of the parish. It was funny to watch; a lot of parishioners sat in the same spot every week, so they would walk in and proceed to what they felt was their reserved seat. There were times, usually around the holidays, when all the C&E Christians, meaning Christmas and Easter attendees, would take a spot usually occupied by one of the weekly members. The looks on their faces showed it all. The look of do you know you're in my seat? They would reluctantly move elsewhere.

The Mass was offered in the usual manner, and Father Dean gave his usual great homily. He spoke loudly and clearly, and his message was always effective. He liked to kid, and implemented a joke or two into his message every week. The parishioners loved it, and him.

After the final blessing and hymn, the congregation exited. Father Matthew, who exited first, stood at the door wishing all a good day. I stood off to the side, waiting to have my audience.

The church was empty now, and Father Matthew and I were seated in the pew in the rear of the church.

"So, Jake, how are you holding up since the loss of Kathleen? I know that losing Kathleen was tough. I would like to know more details of her illness."

"You are correct, Father," I started. "She was my wife of nearly thirty-eight years. Not a day goes by that I do not think about her. She was a beautiful lady with a great smile. She rewarded me with a handsome son, John, and a beautiful daughter, Ann. She was a great mother and wife."

Father Matthew was especially close to Kathleen, because she'd worked as the church secretary for over twenty-five years. Her tenure started long before he arrived, and she had seen many pastors and associate pastors come and go.

I responded in a solemn manner. "Father, Kathleen was the love of my life. I do not know why, but I always thought we would leave this earth together. I know this idea is very impractical, but I just felt we would. You know, Father, I really enjoy traveling. When the children were young, we took a lot of trips and vacations as a family. We traveled all around this country, as far west as Hawaii, south to Florida and north to the New England states, and many states between. We had many wonderful times together as a family. After John and Ann went off to college, we became empty nesters, and I wanted Kathleen and me to go to Italy. It finally happened, and the trip was wonderful."

Every time I was asked about it, I would get so emotional I had difficulty speaking. As I talked, Father Matthew nodded and related to my remarks.

I continued, "We returned home and life was back to normal. Kathleen went back to working at the church rectory, and I assumed my retiree responsibilities of cooking, cleaning, doing laundry, and yard work to make things as easy for Kathleen as possible. Then things started to go downhill. Kathleen's mother, Mary, and stepfather, John, who were both getting up in age, became ill. They were in and out of hospitals and rehab centers. They just could not get well. That was hard for both of them, for they had, for the most part, been healthy active people.

"While this was happening, Kathleen started having problems of her own. Her back began to give her tremendous pain. This caused her to be unable to work, as you are aware. After months of going to various doctors, the problem was finally diagnosed.

"Kathleen and I were visiting Ann and her family for our grandson James's birthday. It was a struggle for Kathleen, but she endured the five-hour ride. She was not going to miss the birthday. As we sat around talking, my cell phone rang. I walked out on the porch to take the call. It was Dr. Mark Capo. He told me that the biopsy that was taken during Kathleen's back surgery showed that she had cancer. Father, it was like somebody punched me in the stomach and knocked the wind out of me. The question now was, how do I tell Kathleen?

"The visit ended and we went to our hotel. I kept the news inside me all that night and slept very little. The next day we went back to Ann's and took part in the party. Kathleen spent most of the time lying down on the sofa, showing love to the grandchildren. When the party was over we said our goodbyes and headed back to the hotel. While riding back, Kathleen looked at me and asked, 'Do you think I have cancer?'

"I looked at her and with much hurt in my heart I had to tell her. 'Do you remember when Dr. Capo called yesterday? Well, I did not lie to you when you asked what he wanted, but I did not tell you the whole story.'

"When I told her, naturally she was devastated and began to cry. We spent the night crying as I tried my best to console the love of my life of nearly four decades. Thus started the journey of many doctor visits and treatments.

"Through it all, Kathleen was strong, and although she was very uncomfortable, she never complained. The diagnosis, after many tests, of pancreatic cancer was the worst news we could have received. Medicine has advanced a long way with some cancer treatment, but this type had no cure. This situation to me was the worst thing in the world, having someone you love incur a problem and not be able to find a remedy. I remember the treatment doctor's words.

"'I will make Kathleen as comfortable as possible so she can get out and around on a limited basis for as long as I can, but I cannot cure her.'

"I did my best, Father, but every day, I think, was there something else I could have done? I know she's in heaven now, comfortable."

"Jake, you did well," Father Matthew responded. "You move on. It is time to make new memories and stop dwelling on the old. Oh my, look at the time. We have chatted for quite a while. I have two more Masses to say today. I better get a move on it."

"Thanks for the concern, Father," I responded.

"Stay strong, Jake. I am a believer in no matter how bleak things seem to be at times, things always seem to work out." With that, Father Matthew walked off to prepare for his next Mass, and I headed home.

CHAPTER 6
THE ADVICE

THE COOL FALL AIR HAD moved into Follansville and for the residents it meant one important thing: it was football season. The season was in full swing and the Blue Riders were undefeated. I followed the team as much as I could, but not as much as I did in the past, when John and Ann were students and I knew a lot of the players. This said, being a former Blue Rider, I always wanted to see them win. I was heading down to Bessie's for my morning coffee. As I approached the diner I heard a voice call for me.

"Hey, Jake, you have a few minutes?"

I turned to see Timmy Bradlee. Timmy was the quarterback on the Follansville football team, and a pretty good one at that. There was a bench in front of Bessie's, and after shaking hands and extending greetings both of us sat down.

"Jake," said Timmy, "I need your advice. The season is quickly coming to a close. Our record speaks for itself and hopefully we can win the state championship."

"So why do you need my advice? Everything seems to be going well for you."

"Jake," said Timmy, "I was not around when you played, but I heard you were a real good player – all valley and all state – and I am sure you had colleges trying to recruit you. This is where I need your advice."

Timmy proceeded. "I am being recruited by schools, but most of them are small schools, Division 2 and 3. Jake, I think I am good enough to play major college football. I want to play Division 1. I know I can get stronger and play better. Coach Willis has not been any help. I received a letter recently from a Division 1 school offering me a scholarship. When I showed it to Coach Willis he seemed surprised. He offered no advice. He just looked at me like he could not believe the letter. Jake, I really need your thoughts."

I pondered, and then spoke. "Timmy, if you think you will be happy at the Division 1 School that is courting you, I suggest you contact them and schedule a visit if you have not been there already. Make sure you'll like it there and that they're really serious about signing you. You are aware these schools only have so many scholarships to offer each year. For them to commit is a major decision for them, as well as for you. Let me end it with this. When I graduated I had offers from Division 1 schools as well as smaller schools. I opted to go to a small school. I started as a freshman and played with some great guys. It was a wonderful experience, but the thought has always lingered in my mind, could I have made it at the Division 1 level? I will never know. You have the chance to answer that question. If you do not try, you will never know. If that's what you want, go for it; be determined to live your dreams."

Timmy looked me in the eye. "Thanks, Jake, you have been a big help."

"No matter what you decide, Tim, rest assured I will follow your career, and I am sure you will be successful. Remember, football is important, but getting a good education is more important. Do not let your studies lag because of football. You can be successful at both, but you will have to put forth a lot of effort. I hope I see you in the pros someday, but if that does not happen, have that sheepskin on your wall so you can get a good job."

Timmy nodded as we shook hands. "I'll keep you posted, Jake."

"By the way," I questioned, "why aren't you in school?"

"No school today, teachers' conference day."

I shook my head. "Oh, I never had those when I went to school."

Timmy really had his mind set on playing Division 1 football. Without him knowing, I was going to try to help. A friend of mine from our playing days named Mike Kelly was a local bird dog for colleges. He would alert schools about athletes that he felt would fit in their programs. I phoned Mike and alerted him to Timmy Bradlee. He told me he was aware of his talent and would make a call or two to see what he could do. He thought Timmy would be a real good fit in the Duke University program. The reason was, Tim was a good student as well as an athlete.

"Mike," I said, "anything you can do I would appreciate. I know Timmy will not let you or the university down. I owe you one."

"Jake," Mike responded, "Anything I can do to help a good young athlete makes my life better."

CHAPTER 7
THE GOOD DAY

I MADE MY WAY INTO Bessie's. The breakfast and turn change crowd were gone and I could have about any booth or table that I wanted. Usually if it was available I sat in the last booth near the wall, facing the counter and all the other tables and booths. I referred to it as the BRD, the back-row delegation, an expression that I'd picked up back in my college fraternity days. There was a small group that liked to sit in the back row of the meeting room. Those that occupied the rear seats used this term or abbreviation and said they preferred to watch everybody rather than have everybody watch them. I reminisced as I thought about my days as a member of the fraternity at State College, or University, which it has since become after I graduated. The crazy fun times that were had were beyond belief.

State was a small school in a small town. The town had one small gas station and general store combined. Next door was a pizza shop that served beer. There was a post office, a church, and an elementary school. No matter what direction you entered the town from you had to travel up a hill. The roads were narrow and winding, and many a night the brothers wondered how they made it home after a night of socializing. On Thursday nights, for example, a lot of the students congregated at The Bucket, or, as it was called in the old days, The Bloody Bucket. Confrontations sometimes occurred after a few beers were drunk, and those involved usually left bloody. The Bucket was a few miles from the campus, and driving was almost a must, but there were times that walking it was attempted.

The Bucket was far from glamorous. It was not the kind of place you would bring your mother when visiting the school. When entering the door from the parking lot the long wooden bar was to the right side of the building with about a dozen stools. On the left side were tables for four with chairs, which sometimes ended up being tables for ten. A narrow aisle way allowed the patrons to proceed to the back room. This was the dance floor as well as mingling area.

Occasionally Bucket Bob, the owner, would supply a so-called band, which was more like guys making noise with instruments. This was very infrequent, so most of the time it was just a loud jukebox supplying the music. Songs like "In the Midnight Hour" and "We Gotta Get Out of This Place" were played, sung, and danced to.

Another means of entertainment was a bowling machine. A puck was used to slide over raised wires. Running over those wires signaled the pins to move in an upward motion like they had been knocked down. The machine tallied the scores, and three hundred games were not unusual. Players would play for beers. The best players, like Charles "Psych" Adelic and Artie Matuska hardly ever had to buy. They knew how to play the game.

I had my head down, kind of daydreaming about the old days, when a voice startled me out of my thoughts. "Hey, horse trader, what are you up to?" I knew by the greeting it was my friend and world's best horse handicapper, Terry Day.

I responded to his greeting, "Always living the dream. What brings you to Bessie's at this hour?"

"I was just riding around in the Mustang" – his reconditioned 1964 model – "and decided to stop at the bus terminal to buy a racing form. I just looked at it briefly, but there are a few races where I have selections that I think will do real well. I am thinking about riding up. Do you want to join me?"

I really did not have anything going that was pressing. "Why not, let's go."

With that we headed up the road to Riverside Downs and Casino. Terry was a good friend and a real gentleman. He did not drink, smoke, or use profanity. He said people that used profanity as a descriptive adjective had poor vocabularies. I hardly ever saw him get upset. It took a lot to get him to that extreme. We both liked the races and had even taken trips together to some of the bigger out-of-town tracks like Saratoga in New York, Gulfstream in Florida, and Churchill in Kentucky.

As we pulled into the parking lot there they were, like sacred monuments, the "Track Cars." These were owned by the everyday attendees. They were usually at least twenty years old or looked it. They were the big cars, the Olds 98s, Cadillac Deville's and the like. They had not been washed in months, it appeared. The back seats were full of old racing forms and the fronts with coffee cups and cigarette butts. There was an occasional cracked windshield, and most of the tires were much worn, but they made it to the track every day.

As we entered the track we ran into Railbird Rudy. Rudy was a fixture at the track. If he was not there you could be sure he was either extremely ill or dead. Rudy was almost always touting a horse or two. The idea was he gave you his selection and you would make a bet for him. If it won he made some money. A loser cost him nothing. In other words, he was a tout. Terry and I were wise to his game.

"I have a sure thing today. You guys want in, Rudy asked?

Terry whispered to me, "Rudy has not had a winner since the eighth-grade picnic."

Terry said, "I tell you what, Rudy, here's a fiveski, go make a bet on your pick. I do not want to know who it is because I might jinx you."

"That is mighty nice of you, Terry," Rudy responded as he walked away to place his wager. As he did he shouted, "You guys will be sorry."

Terry opened the form. "I know who he likes, Mr. Hugh in the next race."

Mr. Hugh had a lot of early speed, but unless the race was three furlongs he did not stand a chance. The race he was entered in today was a five-furlong sprint, which was about two furlongs more than Mr. Hugh could handle.

We sat down to enjoy the show and watch Rudy. He positioned himself at the lower end of the grandstand outside area near the fence. The race went off, and, as was his forte, Mr. Hugh went to the front.

Rudy started screaming, "Come on, Mr. Hugh. Run, boy, you can do it."

As the horses came around for the stretch Mr. Hugh was in front but was starting his usual move to the rear. Rudy started running up the grandstand area trying to urge his selection onto a victory. It was not to be. As a matter of fact, I think Rudy beat Mr. Hugh to the finish line. A despondent seventy-plus senior citizen with thinning gray hair, khaki cargo shorts, black orthopedic shoes, and a white T-shirt walked away dejected. Terry and I laughed.

"Don't worry," said Terry, "he'll have another sure thing tomorrow."

As was his norm, Terry's selections performed well and we both left the track with nice profits. "Not a bad return for the hour or so that we've been here, eh, horse trader?"

"You're the best, Terry. I have always told people that. I think the only thing you may do better than horses is shoot craps."

Terry grinned and spoke. "Since we are up here, do you want to roll the bones for a while?"

"Why not, Ter, you seem to be on a lucky streak today."

We went into the casino and positioned ourselves around a five-dollar-minimum-bet crap table. It was still early and the tables were not busy, thus the five-dollar minimum bet. Once more players began to show at the tables the minimum bets would go up. We watched the table for a while. The shooter with the dice failed to impress. He rolled his point, which he now needed to make again before he rolled a seven. He threw two more rolls and the dreaded seven appeared. Sevens and elevens are good on the first roll, but sevens are not after a point has been established.

The chips were removed from the table and the dice were passed to Terry. He made a conservative ten-dollar bet on the pass line, which allowed him to roll the dice. I made the same bet. As was Terry's technique, as soon as the stickman pushed the dice his way he grabbed two and let them fly immediately to the far end of the table as required. "Seven winner," said the stickman.

Good start, but neither Terry nor I commented on the win. We were hoping for bigger and better. Terry raised his bet on the pass line to twenty dollars. I followed suit. The dice were pushed his way and again they flew quickly. "Eight, easy eight," voiced the man with the stick.

The dice showed a five and a three, thus easy, unlike two fours, which are considered making eight the hard way.

A couple more players joined us at the table and began to make their side bets. Terry and I did the same. We made bets on the five, six, nine, and ten and took odds on the eight. Now all he had to do was roll these numbers and not roll a seven. That is exactly what the master did. It seemed like every roll he rolled a number we had bet or his point.

As Terry won he kept pressing his bets, meaning adding more money to the bets he had made. I upped a little, but I was a more conservative better than my playing partner. It seemed like Terry rolled for twenty minutes before he finally threw the seven. Fortunately just before the seven was rolled we took most of our bets down, so our losses on the seven were minimal. Our billfolds had increased by additional hundreds of dollars. We walked away with smiles on our faces, as did the other players who congratulated Terry on his roll.

"Not a bad day, huh, horse trader? I wish they were all this way."

I agreed, with a "For sure."

Terry drove home and dropped me off at my car at Bessie's. We shook hands and I thanked him for the ride, both in the Mustang and on the ponies and the crap table.

"No problem, buddy. We'll do it again sometime. I'll give you a call. Have a good rest of the night."

"Thanks again, Terry."

CHAPTER 8
THE NEIGHBORHOOD

I THOUGHT TO MYSELF THIS day, you know, as you get older time seems to fly. I remember my parents telling me and my brothers Andrew and David this all the time, but we did not think the days were going that fast. Now that I am my parents' age it seems like Christmas had just passed, and it was nearly upon us again. As was my norm, I was preparing to leave for my place in Florida in a few weeks. The cold weather and I did not get along. Although the weather was still fall comfortable I knew the cold weather with snow, ice, and wind were on this way. I had to go south before this happened. I always said I did not care if I saw another snowflake. If I wanted to see snow I would watch the Weather Channel on the television.

As I drove down the street in my black Mercedes convertible, I had the top down but was stretching it. It was a pleasant day, but really not the right day to have the top down. I was coming up on two of Follansville's landmark spots, Mae Hand Elementary School playground and, right across the street, Tito's poolroom. Mae Hand was a very rich lady who gave a lot of money back in the old days to the town and the school; thus as repayment it was decided that the elementary school would be named after her. Next to the school was a playground. A few swings, a slide, some monkey bars, and an area for the students to run around at recess and lunch. Included in this area was a basketball court. The court contained two baskets. Each was held in place by two steel pipes about six inches in diameter. The umbrella-shaped back boards on each end held the steel rims. There were no nets. The out-of-bounds line on one side of the court was fine, but the other was right up against the school. Mae Hand was the place to be after school and all through the summer. If the temperature allowed, the teams were designated by shirts and skins. There were games played continuously with teams waiting with "We have winners."

It was not unusual to have an injury or two. The number-one rule was you did not go in for a layup unless there was no one anywhere near you. Those that did not heed the rule usually ended up getting slammed into the pipe that held the basket. The shooter was hurting as the opponent voiced, "I got him," meaning he fouled. One or two of these type of incidents convinced the players not to do something stupid like that again.

Many a game was played on the site over the years and everybody that played claimed to be "All Mae Hand," this being one of the best to play there. Over the years there were hundreds that claimed to be "All Mae Hand," but everybody knew who the best were.

I parked the car and watched the young fellows playing on the court for a few minutes and proceeded to walk across the street to Tito's poolroom. Tito's was not a fancy place by any extreme. The building was entered off of Main Street, and as you entered the door you were facing three aged, heavy slate tables. The first table had the pocket design where the made shots would fill one of the six pockets. Once the game ended the players would remove the balls from the pouches and place them on the table to be re-racked. The other two tables had a trough-type system where the balls would roll down into a square-shaped box, thus allowing for them to be removed and racked more easily.

The man in charge of racking the balls as well as collecting the money for the games played was Bob White. Bob was an elderly fellow in his late seven seventies or early eighties who seemed to have worked at Tito's for forever. He was short and frail-looking with thinning gray hair. He always dressed neat with a pair of slacks and a freshly-pressed shirt. He had lost his wife years back and put his time in at the hall for something to do.

When a game ended someone would yell "Rack" and Bob would slowly move to that table and place the balls in the triangular eight-ball rack, collect the money for the game, and play would proceed.

As I entered Tito's this day there was "The Man" practicing by himself on the first table, Giovanni Bartholomew Bono, Uncle John to me. He was the youngest of my mother's brothers, and our age difference was not that great. People did not believe he was my real uncle. To others he was J.B. or in some cases Johnny B. Good, as his name translated from Italian to English. Uncle John to me was one of the smoothest operators around. He was dark tanned with grayish-black hair. He always dressed neat and had keys to quite a few ladies' places in town. He was about six foot tall, which was probably a stretch, and kept himself in shape at about one seventy or one seventy-five pounds. He'd served in the Army right out of high school. It was during this period that the Green Berets became a special fighting force, so Uncle Giovanni enlisted and became a Green Beret. He served in Vietnam and one could guess saw a lot of action in difficult situations. He never talked about it much, only to say he lost a lot of good friends in combat.

On this day as I was chatting with Bob White, J.B. moved gracefully around the table eyeing up his shots. He was good and kept an eye out for those that thought he was not. He would play comers in eight-ball or even get into a nine-ball game with money on the five-ball on nine-ball for whoever made them. Uncle J.B. would always tell me the key to being a good pool player was knowing when to miss.

"You do not always have a shot," he would say, so you would miss, but not give your opponent a shot, either. Most of the rookies would try to pull off an impossible shot. They would miss and Johnny B. Good would run the table.

As J.B. played and Bob and I talked, the door opened and two guys entered who were not familiar to us. They were acting a little cocky and inquired as to when J.B. would be vacating the table. The other two tables were occupied as well.

J.B. replied, "Pal, when I'm finished I will let you know." This did not make the strangers happy.

As Johnny was preparing to hit his next shot one of the two bumped his stick, causing him to miscue. The incident was assumed to be an accident and J.B. continued his play. I was watching as all this was going on and it appeared that these two goons were looking for trouble, and their prey was the wrong guy to mess with. Even though he was concentrating on his shot and acting very cool, Uncle John continued to eye up his annoyers.

A second attack came as one of the two bumped John as he was about to proceed with his shot. They grinned, and that really upset the former Green Beret. With a quick motion he stabbed the butt end of the cue stick into the private area of one of his agitators, and once he bent over in pain, J.B. smashed the smaller end of the cue stick across the shoulder and face of the other. He then continued with a barrage of karate chops and other maneuvers he'd learned in his hand-to-hand combat training. He spun one of the opponents around. I attempted to step in and assist.

"Stay back, Jake. I have this under control."

J.B. continued to punch, kick, and batter both goons with the small and large end of the cue stick, which was now broken in two. The two had had enough and asked for mercy. As John backed off they got to their feet as best they could and wobbled out the door that Bob politely opened for them, saying, "Come back when you learn some manners."

The entire altercation lasted only a minute or two, but a lot of damage was done. The fellows on the other tables were hypnotized at what they had seen. Uncle J.B. thanked me for wanting to help. He brushed himself off and went back to his practicing like nothing had happened. The guy was as cool as they come. I bid Uncle John farewell and said goodbye to Bob as well and headed out the door.

CHAPTER 9
THE MESSAGE

No SOONER DID I HIT the sidewalk than my cell phone rang. I looked at the number and saw that the call was from my son, John. I said hello, and the voice on the other end responded with, "Hey, what are you doing?" which was John's normal initiation of our calls. I told him that I had just left Tito's and was heading toward home. I mentioned the altercation at the poolroom. Once I started the story with the two jerks entering the door, he interrupted by saying, "Let me guess, Uncle J.B. was there and he cleaned their clocks; they messed with the wrong guy."

"Right you are," I responded.

John laughed and replied, "These guys never learn."

John is a great son and I love him and his family very much. He has always made me proud. He is very competitive and hates to lose. He was an Eagle Scout and loved sports. That was usually the topic of discussion in his texts or calls. In his college days he played for the tennis team and was elected president of the fraternity, the same one that I belonged to, and during his senior year was president of the student body. John is my son, brother, and closest confident. He is always ready to help me no matter what the situation.

We talked for a few minutes and he had to run because he was taking Grace and Jack, my much-loved grandchildren, to the park. He said we would talk later via either phone or Face time on the computer. I agreed and ended with "Tell Theresa, my daughter-in-law, hello."

As I returned to the Mercedes I checked the time on my cell phone. Since it was Saturday afternoon I decided to fulfill my obligation of going to Mass at St. Blaise's at four p.m. The ride was very short, only about a mile, and I arrived in no time. As I was entering the church I saw Father Matthew talking to some of the parishioners in the pews, as he would do if time allowed. He saw me and came up to extend a greeting. "How are things, Jake?" He always showed concern for me since the loss of Kathleen.

"I am doing well, Father, and thanks to Rod Reeves, a fraternity brother from my college days, I met a lady who, as you suggested, is helping me make new memories."

"Great!" Father exclaimed. "Do I know her? Is she from town?"

"No," I replied, "but I will be sure to introduce you formally when she's with me. Her name is Jane Ivan. She is a breast cancer survivor. I tell her she is tough, although she says she's not. She has been through a lot in her life, thus I say she is tough. She is a wonderful lady who has been a Godsend. As you know, Father, living alone is not always fun. She and I laugh and have a lot of fun together and spend as much time together as we can. We have taken trips together to Paris and Ireland and have had wonderful times. I will tell you more when time allows. I know you have a Mass to offer."

Mass went on pretty much as usual, with the prayers as well as the two readings that normally proceed the Gospel. Today's Gospel was from Matthew Chapter 7, verses 7 through 12. Father Matthew read, "Ask and you will receive; seek and you will find; knock and the door will be opened to you." He read on, "For everyone who asks will receive and anyone who seeks will find and the door will be opened to him who knocks." The reading concluded with, "Do unto others what you want them to do for you."

After the Gospel reading ended it was time for Father Matthew to begin his sermon. His voice and delivery were very good and the parishioners waited anxiously to hear his message.

"Ask and you will receive; seek and you will find; knock and the door will be opened to you," Father started out, reiterating the reading. "How do you do this? Do you just ask God for his favors and he automatically gives them to you? I just do not see it being that easy."

He continued, "Treat others as you want to be treated. Basically you have to live a good life to earn heaven. Let me describe it this way. When people die, on their stone at the cemetery or mausoleum are dates, the date they were born and the date they died. But more important than these dates are the line or dash that separates them. That mark designates your life. How good a person were you between the day you were born and the day you died? Did you treat people the way you wanted to be treated? Were you good Christians?"

The entire congregation listened attentively to Father Matthew as he brought his sermon to a close. "The date you came into this world is important and the date you leave this world will be noted, but the most important mark on your tombstone will be the dash between them. Will yours be strong enough to earn you eternal happiness?"

With this the Mass continued with singing and prayers, as always, and after the final blessing the service was complete. The congregation left the church and many greeted Father Matthew and voiced their appreciation for the service and offered him hope for a pleasant day. I followed suit in wishing Father a good day and told him I really liked his sermon.

"Thank you, Jake," he replied. "Bring your lady to Mass sometime. I would love to meet her."

"Will do Father," I responded.

CHAPTER 10
THE SCHEME

THE WEEKEND PASSED BY QUICKLY with no dramatic occurrences, but I was not looking forward to Monday. I had my periodic check-up with Dr. Capo. The appointments had been going well, but things come up when you least expect them. I entered the office, said hello to the ladies working in the office, and took a seat. In a short while Dr. Capo's physician's assistant called me back to the treatment room. The first order of business was to be weighed. I removed my shoes and stepped on the scale. As were my usual remarks to her: "Your scale is off, I weighed four pounds less on my home scale this morning."

She would smile and say that she would make a note of it. She proceeded with her routine. Why was I there, any problems? Then she proceeded to take my blood pressure and pulse and check my lungs and heart with her stethoscope. She said all seemed fine and the doctor would be in shortly.

It was not long before the door opened and Dr. Mark Capo entered. "Jake, boy, how are you?"

I replied, "You tell me, Doctor, that's what I came here to find out."

Out of respect I always tried to refer to him as Doctor, not Doc. I felt it was a title that he'd earned, and using slang like Doc did not seem proper. This is something I believe in. Our society has become too liberal and has taken freedom too far. The days of yes, sir; no, sir; yes, ma'am; no, ma'am; please and thank you have somehow lost their place in many people's lives. The same holds true with men taking their hat off during the National Anthem at a sporting event, even after they're asked by the PA announcer to remove them. I was always taught that a gentleman removed his hat whenever entering a building. This was the proper thing to do. Nowadays it seems some men cannot eat a meal out unless they are wearing a baseball cap with a logo of their favorite team or some other trademark. It must make their food taste better.

Dr. Capo and I talked about my condition, which seemed to be in order. "I would like to see you when you return from Florida, Jake; you're doing well now, but I want to keep an eye on you. Are you still doing your swimming at the pool? I hope so. The experts say three to five days a week of some kind of exercise is a good routine to get into. And go easy on the chips and donuts, okay? Let's see if we can get your weight down some, okay? And, Jake, contrary to your comments, my scale is very accurate."

I nodded and felt like the kid who got caught with his hands in the cookie jar. We shook hands and bid farewell to each other. "By the way," Dr. Capo asked, "where are you off to for your next traveling adventure?"

"I'm heading to Florida for the winter months and may try to work in a trip to Spain if I can work out a good deal. A good deal is not always price to me; it is value. What do I get for my money? I always said I would pay twice as much for something if it lasts ten times longer than a competitor." This being said, I headed out the door.

The Mercedes was parked in the lot just outside of Dr. Capo's office. As I opened the door and positioned myself in the seat my cell phone rang. I looked and saw that it was a call from my daughter Ann. My hello was responded to with "Hi, Dad." My usual response would be "Hi, Ann, how are you doing," and as usual, the response was "Goood!"

Ann, or Dr. Annie, as she had become after earning her doctorate in audiology, is a terrific daughter and I love her and her family very much. She is very pretty and, it goes without saying, very intelligent. She graduated in the top twenty of her high school graduating class and was on the honor roll every semester while attending the state university. She continued her ranking during her post-graduate classes while earning her master's degree and then her doctorate.

We chatted, and I as always asked about my handsome and beautiful grandchildren James, Lucy, and Rose. As was the norm, Ann said they were fine. We chatted about what they were into, which usually included baseball, dancing, gymnastics, and school. After a brief chat Ann said she really did not need anything and had just called to check in on me. I replied that I was well and preparing to make my trip to Florida for the winter, and that I hoped she would make it down for a visit. We bid our goodbyes and I started the Mercedes and headed downtown to see what was going on.

As I drove past Bessie's I noticed a few cars in the parking lot and I recognized one belonging to Luke Turkal, so I decided to stop. As I entered he was sitting alone in a booth. Immediately upon seeing me, he stood up and greeted me with, "Amigo, Como esta usted," to which I replied, "Muy bien."

I knew very little Spanish, while Luke was very proficient in speaking, writing, and teaching the language. He even spent time studying at the University of Barcelona in his earlier years, but kindly returned to be best man in my wedding.

"How is my brother from another mother?" I asked. We embraced and both took a seat in the booth. He had a coffee in front of him, and I ordered one as well. Our conversational subjects varied during our get-togethers – lottery numbers, football games, food, restaurants, just to mention some – mostly just routine conversation, but every now and then we would reminisce about some activity in our lives and wonder how we'd gotten into these situations and, better yet, how we'd gotten out of them.

Our conversation this day led us to talk about a New Year's Eve that we'd started celebrating at an early hour, and by the time midnight came neither one of us was in any condition to drive. We were cognizant enough to know that the city police and state troopers would be on the lookout for drunk drivers, and a roadblock would not be out of the question. As luck would have it, when we walked, or should I say staggered, out of the Regal Club there was a taxi parked right in front of the building. We figured the roadblocks would not stop a taxi, and as we expected they waved the vehicle right through.

We arrived at Luke's house, and now the trick was, what were we going to do with the taxi? We were sobering up fast. We pulled into Luke's neighbors' garage, which were out of town, and closed the door. The rest of the night we slept off our beverages. The trick now was returning the taxi. We entered the garage and prayed that we did not confront any police officers while en route to our drop-off location. Since it was New Year's morning traffic was pretty light, and the street had little if any. We parked the taxi close to where we'd borrowed it, on a side street, and ran, hoping no one saw us. No one did. Boy, were we lucky. The things you do not do when you are young. We looked at each other and smiled.

Luke looked at me and said, "The good ol' days, huh, amigo?" I just smiled.

We finished our coffee, paid the check, and headed out the door. "I am going to take a walk down to Moose's to see what kind of scuttlebutt I can learn. Do you want to join me, Luke?"

"Not this time, Jake. I have to get home. My wife, Natasha, is waiting for me. We are going to take a trip out to the Amish country. Looks like it is going to be a nice day, so it should be an enjoyable ride. I will let you know if I find anything interesting."

"You do that. Enjoy your day, Luke. Tell Natasha I said hello."

We parted ways and I headed to my planned destination. Upon entering Moose's place I noticed two of the locals looking over a racing form with the entries for the day's races at Riverside Downs. These guys, oddly enough, were named Rich and Ritchey, and were daily visitors to the Downs.

"Boy, I am glad you guys are here," I voiced. "I bet you two experts have been reviewing the form and have all the winners. How about letting me in on a few."

Rich replied, "They're tough today, Jake. Real competitive races with big fields."

Ritchey seconded the remarks. "Here, take a look."

I glanced down at the paper and scanned the first two races. In the second race there was a horse named Big Double. "Here you go," I said, "Big Double in the second race. I can see the results in the *Review* tomorrow; Big Double wins in Big Double."

Ritchey shot back, "This horse is thirty to one, Jake. He does not stand a chance."

"Really?" I replied. "I will tell you what I am going to do. You guys are going up to the track; are you not?"

"You know we are, Jake," Rich replied.

"Good. Then I want you to make a bet for me. Here's ten bucks. I want you to bet the two early-line favorites in the first race with Big Double in the second. I will meet you here tomorrow about the same time and you can give me my money. If you're smart you'll play at least a two-dollar double for yourselves."

Ritchey looked at me and said, "You know, Jake, I am tempted to book that bet myself. It would be the easiest ten dollars I ever made. Big Double does not stand a chance."

"Don't do it," I replied. "I'd hate for you to have to pay me a grand out of your pocket. Make sure you bet dollar- and two-dollar-max tickets. Just be sure I have five dollars worth of bets on each double. I don't want to do a signer and have to pay taxes on the winnings. See you tomorrow." With that I left.

John Mihalyo

CHAPTER *11*
THE PROFIT

THE NEXT MORNING I AWOKE to beautiful sunshine. After giving thanks to God for allowing me to sleep well through the night and thanks for all the blessings for me and my family, both living and deceased, I started my morning routine. Coffee, a sweet of some sort, and then I proceeded to the television to watch the news. A copy of the morning paper, the *Follansville Review*, was on my front porch. This was surprising to me because I did not subscribe to the paper. I started to page through it and the thought crossed my mind to check the race results for yesterday at the Downs. My eyes moved to the second race and to my disbelief, Big Double had won the race and paid sixty-six dollars to win. My excitement grew and I quickly looked at the first race results. "All right!" I shouted to myself. One of my picks in the first race had won and the daily double paid four hundred and sixty dollars for a two-dollar bet. I could not wait to get to Moose's today and collect my cash. I had over a thousand dollars coming. My blood was flowing now. I finished my coffee and goodie and headed to the shower.

I drove to Moose's at about the same time as yesterday, hoping Rich and Ritchey were there, and keeping my fingers crossed that they'd made the bets for me and hadn't screwed them up. I pulled the convertible in front of the establishment and briskly walked in. There was R and R waiting for me.

"Well, guys," I boasted, "how do you like me now?"

"Jake," Rich said, "you have to be the luckiest man alive."

"Why is that, Rich?"

Ritchey chimed in quickly, "Not only did Big Double win the second race, but in the first race an unbelievable thing happened. Your horse and another horse were coming down the stretch neck and neck. It was going to be a photo finish. Both riders were reaching out for all they were worth trying to urge their mounts to the finish line for the win. Then it happened. Just before they hit the line the rider on the horse you did not bet fell off the horse due to his efforts. Thus your horse won the race. In all my years of going to the races I have seen some really bizarre things, but this one took the cake. Then to have your thirty to one shot win the second race, unbelievable."

I shot back, "That's horse racing, boys. The race is not over until it is official."

Rich handed me the winnings, $1,150. I asked, "Did you guys bet a ticket?"

They looked down in shame. "Nope."

"Not even two bucks between the two of you?" I asked with excitement. "Four dollars would have brought you back four hundred and sixty to split."

"You're right, Jake; we messed up," came the reply.

The boys felt bad. I gave each of them a C-note out of the winnings, plus another fifty for lunch, which I knew would go through the mutual windows.

"Hey, thanks, Jake," Rich replied. "That is awful nice of you."

"Hopefully that will be seed money for today. I am sure you're going to make the trip again." Both were a little happier as they nodded.

"Well, good luck. I am out of here, I have things to do. I am getting ready to head south soon and the money will come in handy."

I left Rich and Ritchey, got back in the car, and headed to Follansville Savings and Loan. I had to make a deposit. As I entered, the bank was not busy and a few of the tellers were quick to wave and say hello.

"Who wants to go to work?" I asked. All of the girls were quite friendly and always did a good job. I obtained gift envelopes to send checks to all five grandchildren so they could take part in my good fortune. I made calls to John and Annie, telling them the story and letting them know that the checks were coming. They both thanked me and said they would keep an eye out for the mail.

"Make sure they get treats with some of the money "Pap" sent, okay?"

They both said they would.

What a day, and it was only half over. I might have to play the lottery. Maybe the stars were aligned for me now; maybe my luck would continue. I kept thinking about my good fortune. It was nice to have some unexpected cash. As I pondered what had happened I thought, this is nice, Jake, but what is really important in life is your health. God has blessed me. I feel good and hope to continue to feel good. You can be the richest man in the world, but if your health fails and you die, what good are your material things on earth? We all know we are going to leave this earth some day and we all get a turn. The most important thing is to always be ready spiritually, pray often and, as was written in the reading from Matthew at the weekend Mass, "Ask and you shall receive." It is not automatic. God wants all of us to be with him in heaven, but we all have to do our part.

I thought back years ago to when I taught Bible school on Sundays. My group was usually seventh or eighth graders. I had an exercise I did with them. I asked them, if they went to the doctor and he told them they only had a week to live, what would they do? They thought and eventually got around to the most important element, to be prepared spiritually to get into heaven, to ask God for forgiveness, and if they were sincere they would receive what they asked for. Then came my big point.

"Are you all sure you will be here next week? None of us know, so the important thing is to be ready to leave this earth at any time. Ask God every day for forgiveness and work hard each day like it is your last, so that if it is you will enjoy the Kingdom of Heaven."

John Mihalyo

CHAPTER 12
THE WINNERS

I CRANKED UP THE MERCEDES and headed for the health club to get some exercise in by swimming laps in the pool. I found swimming to be a good workout and it was a lot easier on my knees and back. I parked the car in the lot for the club, which also served as a parking lot for the local baseball teams of all age groups. I walked over to the fence and watched some of the activity. There was quite an array of teams and age groups. Everybody from five- and six-year-old T-ballers to older more experienced pony-league-age players. The little ones were very entertaining. They seemed so small. It was hard to believe I'd coached my son, John, on a team with youngsters such as what were on the field. I could not believe him and his teammates were that small?

I was made aware of one big difference today for some of the age groups. No score was kept. The players batted, ran bases, and played in the field, but since no score was kept nobody won or lost. As I watched I thought about another one of my "isms," as I call them. It is great that children participate in sports, but there is one part of the game that, as in life, they must learn. Everyone wants to win, but that does not always happen.

I observed these youngsters, one of which could grow up to be president of the United States someday. I felt they should be taught how to celebrate when you win and how to learn the disappointment if you lose. Yes, I realized they were young, and when they came up short was a great time for Mom or Dad to put an arm around them and tell their son or daughter they'd played well, but they'd have to keep working hard to get better so in the next game they would be victorious. Usually a stop at the ice cream shop after the game would help immensely to get over the disappointment of a loss.

The same holds true in academics in high school. I read the *Review* and it was noted that Follansville High School had five valedictorians and six salutatorians. In my mind this was not possible. I knew all of these students were very intelligent, but somebody had to be just a little more knowledgeable than the rest. The fact that these students went through four years of high school and earned the exact same skill level in every subject was hard to believe. Just like in sports, somebody wins and somebody loses or comes in runner-up. There is only one championship team, just as one should be valedictorian and one should earn salutatorian. All participants, whether it is sports, academics, or just living your life, try hard, but most of us will agree we probably could have put out just a little more effort. That extra push could have won a championship or a higher ranking scholastically.

My thoughts had taken me away from my reason for being in the area. To the pool, Jake, I thought. These pounds are not going to just disappear. If only things likes ice cream, donuts, and cake kept you thin and healthy, and foods like wheat germ, broccoli, and kale made you fatter and unhealthy that would be great, but as we know this is not the case. Then in I went, lap one, only half a mile to go.

I splashed my way through the pool and accomplished my goal. The routine did not get any easier the older I got. A steam bath and shower would help ease the body aches. The time had come to get home and relax.

John Mihalyo

Chapter 13
The Invitation

I HAD NOT BEEN HOME more than a few minutes when my phone rang. The voice on the other end after my hello came back, "Hey, Number One, what are you up to?"

"You know me always livin' the dream."

I immediately recognized the voice of my good friend Ken Howell. Ken was an attorney. He'd graduated from law school and started a practice with two of his classmates, William Dewey and David Cheetem. They had a very successful practice, but Ken decided to join the corporate ranks and became a contract lawyer at Follansville Steel. I do not remember exactly how we met, but I was sure horse racing had something to do with it. We have continued to be good friends for many years.

Ken continued, "Did you forget what is happening at the end of the month? It is high holy weekend for horse-racing enthusiasts, Breeders' Cup, and you should be elated to know I have a ticket for the weekend that has your name on it. Are you available?" Ken asked.

Ken and I had attended many Breeders' Cups together all over the country. This year it was to be held at

Churchill Downs in Louisville, Kentucky. Even though I was making plans to head south, I could push them back a few weeks and take Ken up on his offer. Ken and I always had great times in all of the cities we attended the races. Belmont Park in New York, Gulfstream Park in Florida, and even Monmouth Park in New Jersey, where it rained so hard we ended up watching the races at a casino in Atlantic City.

I thought it over while we made idle chatter. The arrangements were made. Ken had a car rented, a hotel reserved, and the tickets.

"Come on, Jake," Ken exerted, "I will buy you a Bloody Mary," which was our custom on Breeders' Cup day. "I will even give you a program with the winners in it." This was another one of our customs when we bought programs from the sellers. We would ask for a program with the winners in it. This was said jokingly. Of course the winners were in the program, you just had to find them. We did get strange reactions, however, from the program sellers.

I could not say no. "Okay, counselor, I'm in."

CHAPTER *14*
THE SOLUTIONS

ANOTHER DAY, ANOTHER BEAUTIFUL FALL morning. I went through my usual routine, prayers, coffee, news of the world on television, and then to the shower. I did some light housecleaning and laundry. Once these chores were completed it was past midday and I headed downtown to see what problems were being solved by the local experts. I stopped at Stan's barber shop. Stan and his patrons had all the answers to all the world's problems.

As I walked in I was greeted by Stan and the person occupying the chair, Lew Valentine. "How the heck are you, Jake?" Stan asked.

"Always living the dream, Stan, how about you?"

I realized after asking that question I was in for a long dissertation about everything that was wrong in town as well as the state and, of course, Washington, D.C. Stan rambled.

"These politicians do not care about the average Joe; they are only worried about themselves and getting re-elected. Those jobs were not supposed to be lifetime positions. Our founding fathers only intended for an individual to serve for a limited time, implement their ideas, and then move on. There should be term limits for congressmen, senators, and even the Supreme Court. Some of these Supreme Court judges are up there in age. Their best days are behind them, they should move on."

Stan was on a roll. I'd really set a fire under him today. He finally stopped to take a breath and Lewis started. "You know, Jake, it is not any better in the plant. The people running the plant have no idea what is going on. When you were there in charge things were a lot better."

Lewis was one of the employees who worked in the department I managed in Follansville Steel.

"Thank you for the compliment, Lewis. What is going on currently that is you causing you grief?"

"Jake, I'm a good worker, you know that. I always did my job as close to one hundred percent as I could. I remember you telling us at a team meeting that as soon as every guy does their job, not anybody else's, just theirs one hundred percent, you would get rid of every foreman in the place. Well, I tried, but not everybody did. They still had to be told what to do. Thus, the supervisors never went away."

"So what are you doing now, Lewis?" I asked.

"Oh, they have me sanding the buggy track."

"What's wrong with that?" I asked. "It has to be done as part of the overall operations. Every job is important or it would not be there. Don't you understand? I could have the best rolling crew in the world, but if you do not perform your duty as a sander and the buggy delivering the steel to the mill does not stop because of grease on the track, having the best crew does not help. So you see, Lewis, your job, as menial as you feel it is, is important."

Stan tapped Lewis on the head lightly as he finished up. "You got that, Lewis? Every job is important no matter how trivial people feel it is. So as long as it is there, keep striving for the hundred percent. That is what they pay you to do. How would you feel if I only cut seventy-five percent of your hair?"

Thus, the education for the day. When you walk in the doors at Stan's shop you never know what you will learn. All the problems of the world could be solved easily, but unfortunately those who know how are too busy cutting hair or having their hair cut.

Lewis seemed kind of worked up so I invited him over to the Regal Club to have a drink. We entered the dimly lit room, which was only illuminated by lights over the mirrors on the wall behind the bar and some signs advertising a variety of beverages. The only windows were two small openings on either side of the doors. Eddie the bartender greeted us.

"Welcome, gents, what are you drinking?"

Eddie was a good guy and a good bartender. He always had a good word for all the patrons, but he was not afraid to set someone straight if they got out of line.

"Lewis and I are celebrating today, Eddie. Give us two single-malt scotches, Macallan if you have it. I'm buying."

Lewis gazed at me in surprise. "Single malt? What did you do, Jake, hit a number?" He was referring to the fact that single malt was a much pricier drink. It was also my drink of choice.

We toasted to the old days and the times we spent together in the plant. "Lewis, you guys did the work. Your job was to make me look good. The safer you worked the better quality and production you put out, made me look like a great manager. I just tried to make decisions to make your job easier and more efficient. I know there were times decisions were made that for whatever reason did not work out. Just remember the words of Einstein: 'If you never made a mistake you never tried anything new.'"

Lewis and I finished our drinks and shook hands as we bid farewell and exited the club. The afternoon was still young, so I took the opportunity to go to the health club for a swim, a steam bath, and a shower. I always carried my gym bag in the car so as to be prepared if I had the urge to burn off a few calories in the pool. I wanted to take the opportunity because the upcoming weekend was my trip to Kentucky for the Breeders' Cup with Ken Howell, and I doubted that swimming would be part of my agenda. It would be more like beer, Bloody Marys and food, along with lots of betting.

CHAPTER 15
THE TRIP

THE SOUND OF A COUNTRY music song echoed in my ear from my clock radio. The alarm was set for four thirty a.m. I, like most who are awakened at this early hour, rolled over hoping I had set the time incorrectly on the clock. There was no such luck. Ken had said that he would pick me up at five thirty so I had to get moving.

I staggered out of bed and moved slowly to the bathroom to prepare for the day. I proceeded with my morning ritual of cold water on my face, and this was followed by a two-minute brushing of my teeth as per my dentist, Dr. Steiner. Then it was in and out of the shower, a shave, and donning my togs for the day. Since it was going to be a fairly long ride I tried to dress comfortably. Ken had reserved our rooms, so if changing was necessary we could do so quickly before going to the track.

My bag was packed, so after making the bed and straightening up a bit I headed to the kitchen for a coffee. I needed something strong today so the choice was dark roast. I put the coffee in my to-go cup and sipped it slowly while waiting for Ken. A toot of the horn sounded as the rental SUV pulled up in front of my house. Ken stepped out with his traditional Breeders' Cup sweatshirt on that would be his uniform of the day, along with his black pants and white-and-black high-top basketball shoes. I did not know when he'd bought the shirt, but it seemed like every year we went to this event he wore it. Like most horse players he was superstitious.

As I carried my suitcase and coffee to the car I commented, "Nice shirt."

"Hey," he replied, "this is my lucky shirt. You just wait and see, Number One."

Number One was a moniker Ken gave me years ago, signifying I was the best handicapper in the business. I wish it were true.

Ken had rented the car, but if he had a drink or two the deal was I had to drive. There would be no DUIs for the counselor, which was very wise on his part.

The sun was not up but we were on our way. There was not much traffic at this early hour, and Ken was willing to drive for a while, which was fine with me. While on our trip we talked about a lot of topics. The biggest was the upcoming races and who we thought would be the best betting opportunities. Ken had purchased a racing form the day before and had a chance to look over the past performances. As soon as the sun came up and it became bright enough to see the racing form we started to review each race. He told me who he liked, and I chimed in if I saw something that jumped out at me. The analysis went on until we had them all figured out, we hoped.

The ride seemed to go quickly with our talking about our upcoming wagers. It always seemed so easy. This would be our year; we were going to make a bundle. But we said that every year.

"Number One," Ken said, "I feel good this year. We're going to have a fun time and make a lot of money."

To him I responded, "I hope you're right."

So with that the form was put aside and we started to talk about some other issues in the world and what we would do to remedy them.

We got to the topic of taxes. I put forth one of my "isms" to Ken. "I think we should have a procurement tax. Whatever you earn you take home, no taxes are deducted from your paycheck; revenues to the country and the state are obtained by what each individual spends. You establish a percentage rate, fifteen, maybe twenty percent. Everything you buy, from a pack of gum to a new car, this percentage is added to the price. The federal government gets so much, the state gets so much, and so much goes to Social Security. Part of the state's share goes to the cities. There would be no need to file taxes. What do you think about that idea, Ken?"

Ken listened as I rambled. He looked at me out of the side of his eye and spoke. "It sounds so simple on the surface, but I am sure there are a lot of variables that come into play that you're not aware of, Jake."

I came back with, "I would love to put this on the table of some real intelligent economist and let them tell me why it would not work. At least this way the rich would pay their share."

We had been riding for a while and it was time for a break. Having driven this route many times before, we knew of a sandwich and pastry shop that we were nearing and made that our temporary destination. We used the restroom and purchased a breakfast sandwich, pastry, and coffee. We ate our food; we took the balance of our coffees, and were on our way. There was a driver change as well. I took over the duties of driving, enabling Ken to relax. We began discussing the topic of immigration. Both Ken and my grandparents had come over from a foreign country. We both agreed that immigration was a way of life in our great country, but it had to be done legally. This was the way our loved ones came in, through Ellis Island or some other port of call. We have immigration laws in our country and they have to be upheld. If they're outdated or need adjustment, it is up to our members of Congress and the Senate to make some changes. It will be difficult, and you're never going to please all the people all of the time.

"You know what, Ken? I used to say I could go into a roomful of people and hand everybody a twenty-dollar bill and someone would complain because theirs was wrinkled."

Ken showed a small grin. "People are funny," he exclaimed. "Everybody wants to march to his or her own drum, thus making the parade of life very noisy and out of step."

The noon hour approached as we neared Churchill Downs. We had been to the track before and were familiar with the parking arrangements. Some of the locals had established a car-parking business. They would advertise the price, and once an agreement was made the businessmen would sit on the hood of your car and direct you to the lot of choice. The nearness to the track had a definite bearing on the price of the transaction.

We parked the SUV, paid the fee, and once we made sure we had all of our essentials we headed in for a day of wagering.

I often referred to the track as a bank, and that I never lost. Some days I would deposit my money through the mutual windows and some days I would withdraw; thus, I never lost. The money was always there.

We purchased a beer and sat down to plan our strategy. The first thing I did was call the person who in my opinion is the number-one handicapper in the world, Terry Day. There was no doubt that he had been reviewing the races, and I wanted his input. The phone rang and Terry answered with, "Hey, horse trader, are you there yet?" He was aware Ken and I were attending the races.

"We just pulled in a short time ago, Terry, and I wanted to get some selections from you since you're the best."

Terry quickly went through all the races, giving me his selections. I closed with, "Thanks for the help, my friend, and good luck."

He responded, "Yep, and the same to you guys."

In looking over Terry's choices we saw that we all liked some of the same picks. There were some races where we'd narrowed our choices to one of two horses and there were others where we had a tough time choosing. Ken came up with a strategy.

"Hey, Number One, what about this. Let's split some pick threes starting in the first race." The idea was to choose the winner in races one through three. Then start with the second race and try to do the same in races two through four and so on. The plan was to play the one or two horses that we liked in a race, and the races that we were not sure we would bet them all. Since we were splitting the one-dollar bet most of the races would cost us twenty to thirty dollars per bet each, depending on the size of the fields of the race we played them all.

I agreed with Ken's idea. "Let's give it a whirl and see what happens."

We selected two horses in the first race and two horses in the second race and bet all in the third. One of our selections in the first race won. We were off to a good start. We followed up with a winner in the second, thus guaranteeing us a winning ticket. We had also started a new pick three in the second race with our two selections. We played the entire field in the third and used two selections in the fourth. Our hope now was that a long shot would win in the third race, giving us a bigger win. That is exactly what happened. The horse that won the third race won at twenty to one odds. The pick three paid close to four hundred dollars, and if one of our selections won the fourth race we had another winning ticket.

Ken's idea was working great. We hit four pick threes for the day and each of us made about fifteen hundred dollars. Not a bad start to the weekend. The races ended and we went to our hotel to relax. We freshened up and went out to dinner. After dinner we were tired so we returned to the hotel and turned in for the night. Tomorrow would be another challenge.

We tried our same strategy on Saturday, but our luck was not as good. We did hit two pick threes, which after our bets for the day only netted us a couple of hundred each. We had an enjoyable day withdrawing at "the bank."

On Sunday morning I awoke, went to Mass, returned to the hotel, and met Ken for breakfast before we headed home. Another Breeders' Cup was in the books for the dynamic duo. We headed back home and discussed a multitude of topics. As we talked I decided to question Ken about the judicial system, being that he was a lawyer.

"You know, Ken, I think all lawyers should get rid of all their law books in their offices and hang up the Ten Commandments. You exclude the first four relating to God and religion, and the rest are the law. Think about it. Honor your father and your mother, to include your siblings, show them no disrespect or malice. Thou shalt not kill. You kill somebody except in the case of self-defense, you are guilty. You cannot steal. You steal, you're guilty. You cannot bear false witnesses or lie against your neighbor or anybody else. Imagine how this would affect the politicians. Lastly, you cannot covet your neighbor's goods or his wife. Well, what do you think? These rules have been around since the thirteenth or fourteenth century B.C.

Ken responded back, "Come on, there is more to it than that."

"Oh, really?" I came back. "That is the problem with the system. There are too many loopholes. Trial lawyers try to muddy up the water to get their clients off, even if they know they committed the crime. We have to keep it simple. You kill somebody other than in self-defense for yourself or your family, you're guilty."

I knew my "ism" was extreme, but if you really thought about it, it had merit. There is a correlation between the Commandments and the law. Unfortunately in this day and age law books are permitted in the court; the Ten Commandments are nowhere to be found.

Ken was driving and he glanced over quickly with, "You and your 'isms.'" I just smiled.

Finally, after six hours of driving and a brief rest stop, we arrived at my house. Ken and I bid each other farewell with my comment, "We'll do it again next year, Good Lord willing."

Ken replied that he was in and was looking forward to next year. "I will try to perfect my system," he said.

John Mihalyo

CHAPTER *16*
THE BIRTH

MONDAY MORNING SEEMED TO GET here quick. It seemed like I'd no sooner put my head on the pillow than I was out. The next thing I knew it was eight a.m. and the sunlight was coming through the window. It took a little effort but I rolled out of bed to start the day. As I was drinking my coffee my phone rang. After my hello the voice on the other end came back with, "Hey, what are you doing?" Son John was checking in on me, as was his practice periodically. I looked at the clock and it was a little past nine a.m.

"I am just getting moving. Ken and I drove back from Kentucky yesterday after our weekend at the Breeders' Cup. I was worn out from the pace we set. I am not as young as I used to be."

"I got you," replied John. "You notice I waited until after nine to call you. I know your nine-to-nine rule, no calls before nine a.m. and no calls after nine p.m., unless it is an emergency."

"Thanks for remembering," I responded.

John continued, "Did you guys do any good?"

"We did real well on Friday," as I explained Ken's new system that worked well. " Saturday we did not as well. Made a little money, but Friday was our big day. We made enough to cover all expenses and still have some cash left over. It was a good weekend."

"I am glad you guys did okay," was John's response.

I inquired about Grace and Jack.

"They are doing well," John came back. He continued, "Well, I'll let you go; just checking in. I'm at work, so I better earn my money. I need to put bread on the table for my family, and I'm not a handicapper like you and Kenny. I will text you to set up a Face time this week."

"I will look forward to it," I responded. With that the call ended.

I sat back in my recliner, drinking my coffee with my mind on John and his family, and I started to think about the day Grace, John and Theresa's oldest, was born. My wife Kathleen had received a call that Theresa was getting close to her delivery date, so she and her mother decided to go down a few days early to give assistance if needed. Kathleen told me she would call me when Theresa went into labor. I had a bag packed and was ready at short notice to make the four-hour drive. The call came early in the morning that it was time, so I immediately prepared myself and began the journey so as to be there for the arrival of what I was told would be a granddaughter. I did not know what name had been chosen for her, as John and Theresa wanted it to be a surprise.

It was a gloomy morning. It was not great for driving, especially through the mountains. It would rain some, and then the fog would roll in for a period. These types of conditions made the drive difficult. Then a strange occurrence happened. I had been driving for about three hours and all of a sudden for a brief moment the clouds parted and a ray of sunshine came through. When this occurred I had a flash in my mind – "Grace." John and Theresa were going to name their daughter and my granddaughter Grace. The sunshine only lasted a short period and the clouds came back, along with some rain and periods of fog.

I finally reached my destination, the hospital where the birth was taking place. As I walked in, Kathleen, her mom, and Theresa's mom and dad, Maria and Bob, were waiting to go into the room to see the little one who had been born about an hour ago. This coincided with the ray of sunshine I encountered while driving.

I greeted everyone as John exited from the delivery area. Everyone congratulated him as he told us Theresa and the baby were doing fine. I pulled John aside and quickly told him my story on the trip down and said to him, "You are going to name the baby Grace, right?"

He did not want to give the news up to everybody until Theresa was present, but he gave me a quick nod.

God works in strange ways. I had no idea of the chosen name, but for that short moment I'd received a message. I put down my coffee cup and I paused, as I do often in my day, to give thanks to God for all he had given to me.

After spending a few days with the newborn I returned home. The next day I worked around the house for awhile. There was not a lot to do, being as I had not been there for a weekend. I did some laundry and after finishing the last load in the dryer the clothes were folded and stored back in the dresser.

CHAPTER 17
THE CONVERSATIONS

SINCE I HAD BEEN AWAY I was out of the local gossip loop so I decided to head downtown to see what was happening in the big city. I slid gently into the Mercedes and drove into town. The first stop was Bessie's and the first person I saw was Father Matthew. He was sitting alone nursing a cup of coffee. His mind seemed to be elsewhere.

"Hello, Father."

"Hey, Jake, how are you doing?

"Always living the dream, Father. You know me, everything is Jake."

The term Jake was an expression used in one of my favorite movies, The Sting, with Paul Newman and Robert Redford and Robert Shaw. When things were well they used the term "Everything is Jake." Thus my name went from John to Jake with my friends.

I said hello to Bessie, who was behind the counter, and asked Father, "Do you mind if I join you?"

"I'd love to have some company. I do not have a lot of time, but I will make time for you, Jake."

I ordered a coffee and we started chatting about various topics, but most of the discussion was concerning things that went on at St. Blaise's. Father pointed out that there were nearly fourteen hundred families registered at the parish, but he was lucky to see fifty percent of them at Sunday Mass.

"Those that attended are very faithful," he said, "but I wish I could get the other fifty percent to join us."

"I am with you, Father. I do not think these people stop and realize how lucky they are with all God has given to them. Most of them have good-paying jobs at the plant or are retired with decent pensions and/or Social Security, their houses should all be paid for, they drive nice cars, and for the most part Follansville is a safe area to live in, thanks to the fine job our local law enforcement personnel perform."

Father nodded and I continued, "You are aware, Father, I taught Catholic Christian Doctrine, CCD, to seventh and eighth graders for many years. I had an exercise I would do with them. I would ask them, 'How many hours in a day?' They quickly responded, twenty-four. I followed up with 'How many hours in a week?' This took some calculating time, but they arrived at 168."

I went on, "The Commandments ask us to keep holy the Sabbath; in modern terms, attend Mass on Saturday afternoon or Sunday. We're asked to spend one hour per week minimum to visit God's house and give thanks for all that we have, nice home, nice clothes and food on the table. We take these things for granted, but there are people in this world that have nowhere near what we have. I saw the students' eyes staring and thinking. God asks for less than one percent of our week, more would be great, but a minimum of one percent. I do not feel that is too much to ask, I explained. I hope that lesson stuck to at least some of my students, Father."

"I like that story, Jake. I may have to use it in one of my sermons."

"I hope it increases attendance for you and I hope they show up on time. Those that show up tardy week after week disrupt the congregation. It is nice that they make the effort to attend, but you would hope they would leave just a little earlier to get to the service from the start. I always wonder what time they would show up if their flight for vacation was leaving at ten a.m."

Father just shrugged his shoulders. "You won't make me pay a royalty fee to use your story, will you?" as he chuckled.

"It's on the house," I replied with a smile.

Father Matthew looked at the large round clock in Bessie's and decided it was time to be on his way.

"Have a good day, Father. The coffees are on me."

In his humorous way he responded on his way out that if he knew I was buying he would have ordered a big breakfast to go with the joe. With that, out the door he went.

I gave Bessie a hug, which she returned to me, with, "You know I love you, Jake."

"Thanks, Bessie," I responded as I smiled at her and made my way out the door.

I had not been to Moose's for some time so I decided to stop in and see what was going on. I walked in and saw the crew of Moose, Louie the Greek, Rich, and Ritchey sitting around the card table in a heated conversation. Moose spoke out with, "Jim Brown was the greatest running back of all time. He was tough. Everybody on the defense knew he was going to get the ball, and they were out to get him. He would carry the ball, get tackled, and slowly get back up as if to be hurt. The Browns would line up for the next play, and guess who carried the pigskin? Jim Brown. And he would run as hard as ever. Look at his stats. He was the all-time rusher in the National Football League for years with over twelve thousand yards, and he only played ten games per year for nine years, not fourteen or sixteen like they do now. Yes, Jim Brown was the best."

Louie chimed in after Moose gave up the floor. He spoke in his low, slow voice. "I liked Gale Sayers, the 'Kansas Comet.' The guy was great. He carried the ball from scrimmage, ran back, punts, and kickoffs if needed, and was a good pass receiver out of the backfield. He is my choice."

Rich and Ritchey, who seemed to agree on everything, opted for Emmitt Smith. They were biased, being that for whatever the reason they were both Dallas Cowboy fans. Moose brought that to their attention. "The guy was good, but you two just went with him because he was a Cowboy."

They came back with, "Come on, Moose, he played fifteen seasons and broke the all-time rushing record and led Dallas to three Super Bowls. What's not to like?"

They looked up at me standing in the doorway taking in the expertise. "How about you, Jake," Louie asked, "Who did you like?"

I responded with, "Tony Dorsett. The guy always seemed to run so smoothly, whether he ran up the middle or around the end. He ran effortlessly and never seemed to run any faster, but teams had problems catching him. He played twelve years in the NFL and gained well over twelve thousand yards. Look what he did in college while at the University of Pittsburgh against Notre Dame. I believe he gained three hundred-plus yards in the 1975 game and over seven hundred for a career against the Irish. The Irish were not sorry to see him go pro."

I continued, "The fact is all those guys were great players in their time, but the game has changed. There is more passing now, the blocking rules have changed, there are indoor stadiums so fewer games are played on muddy fields with cold temperatures. There is one thing I think we all agree on. The players today are bigger, faster, and all around better athletes, but the old timers were meaner. They played rough. No helping the opposing player up, no pats on the butt during the game and no theatrics after making a play. They just did the job they were paid to do, and their pay was nowhere near what today's players earn.

"Let me give you an example. If a wage earner in this country averaged fifty thousand per year for the past thirty years, they would have earned one and a half million dollars. There are many players in the National Football League today that make a million or more per year. I know the average lifespan of a player is short. So let's say he plays three years at one million per year. He has earned three million dollars, which is twice as much as the average person would have made over thirty years. Then if they desire they can find employment elsewhere, hopefully with a college degree. They will only be in their mid twenties. Yes, pro football is a rough sport, and the risk of a serious injury is high, but it pays very well. A player who has the opportunity to play in the National Football League has to make a decision: 'Do I risk serious injury for the money, or do I find employment like the average person?' If he goes for the bucks and obtains a serious injury he has no one to blame but himself.

"Playing pro football is physical, and no matter how many years a player plays he will most likely have injuries that will hamper him for the rest of his life. I know the NFL is big business. The gladiators fight each other every week for the crowd in the Coliseum, and the royalty is in the private boxes. The strong will survive and the weak will die. We need not to worry, though, there is always another person wanting to put on the equipment, thus the show goes on, to the joy of the throngs."

I realized I had ranted for a good while. "Sorry, guys," I said, "I was on my soapbox a little too long. As for your choices, all were great. I would take any of one of them on my team."

"Hey, no problem, Jake," said Louie, "it is what it is."

I bid farewell to the group and headed out the door. I left Moose's and headed back to Bessie's, where I was going to meet a guy about doing some consulting work. After I retired I'd started a consulting company, hoping to be able to assist people or small companies to utilize what I had learned over the years in management in the steel industry. I was informed by a mutual friend who asked if we could get together that his name was William Bundle. He was starting up a scrap business not too far from Follansville. I agreed to meet with him as a favor to my friend, but had heard some rumors from others in the industry that he might not be one to work with. The meeting was scheduled for two o'clock at Bessie's. As was my norm, I always made every attempt to be prompt, and most of the time I was early.

I sat in the back booth facing the door, watching for a new face that I would presume to be Mr. Bundle. The meeting time passed and nearly a half hour later my cell phone rang.

"Jake," the voice said, "This is Bill Bundle. What time is our meeting?"

I responded, "You were supposed to be here at two o'clock. It is now two thirty. When can I expect you?"

Bundle's voice came back in a tone like everything was good. He acted like I had nothing better to do but sit at Bessie's and wait for him to get here. I did not like his demeanor on the phone and made up my mind that this potential relationship was not going to go well.

"Mr. Bundle, unless you can be here in about five minutes, our meeting is off." I continued, "Do you know what I hate worse than waiting?"

He voiced back, "No," to which I replied, "Nothing."

The other end of the phone went silent. No apology or explanation for his tardiness. For all I knew he could have been on some golf course. I concluded our conversation.

"Mr. Bundle, I do not think we will be able to work well together. I suggest you find someone else to answer your questions regarding your startup. Have a good day." And with that I ended the call.

I finished my cup of coffee at Bessie's and talked to a few of the folks who were doing much the same. I bid a good-bye to my fellow coffee drinkers and exited

Bessie's. I lowered myself into the car and within a few seconds I was on my way home. The drive was short and within fifteen minutes I was pulling into my driveway. I activated the garage-door opener and pulled the car inside the single-car opening. Up the stairs I went and turned on the television and selected the business channel to see how the stock market was performing. The numbers flashed green, which meant the Dow Jones Industrial Average was up. I was always happy to see green numbers. Green numbers usually meant people's portfolios were getting bigger. This was especially important for retirees from the plant who had little or no defined pensions.

At one time the benefits at Follansville Steel were tremendous. Along with their pensions, the employees had one hundred percent coverage for health care, prescriptions, glasses, dentistry, as well as an insurance policy paid for by the company. Unfortunately, as the years passed and the company started to struggle, many of these benefits were taken away. Those who did have defined pensions had theirs frozen. This meant that no matter how long they worked their pension would not get any larger. Once the company was bought out by the new owner the defined pensions were replaced by a 401 plan. The employees, if they desired, paid into the plan and the company would match a certain percentage. Thus, if the market went up, the employees who participated had a bigger nest egg, at least for that day.

As I sat in my recliner watching the market report my phone rang. I glanced at the screen and noticed my daughter Ann was calling. As usual after my "Hello," Ann replied with, "Hi, Dad," to which I replied with my usual, "How you doing?" To that, Ann came back with "Goood!"

Ann always checked in on me at least once or twice a week to make sure I was okay. She told me that the grandchildren were doing fine and were staying busy with their usual post-school activities. We made some small talk and Ann had to end the call because she was picking up the children at school.

"Okay. Tell James, Lucy, and Rose that Pap says hello and loves them. Tell my son-in-law Jim hello as well. I will talk to you again in a day or two."

It was tough having my children and grandchildren many hours from Follansville. I visited them as much as I could, usually for the grandchildren's birthdays, Thanksgiving, or Christmas. As much as I missed seeing them more often, I always urged John and Ann to live their lives the way they felt best. If they asked me about an issue I would give them my feelings, but the decision was theirs, and not to worry about me, I would be just fine.

One bit of advice I did give them when they were younger went something like this: I would say to them, "You know I like good things, right? I like good food, good drink, nice clothes, nice cars, and great vacations, just to mention a small group. I would tell them these are good things. I do not pass on things that are good. The one thing that I do not do is drugs. If drugs were good for me I would be using them because I like good things."

They both heard the message loud and clear.

John Mihalyo

CHAPTER 18
THE REMINISCING

WHILE SITTING IN THE LIVING room as my eyes panned the area my attention was directed to my photo album from my trips to Europe. These photographs brought back great memories. I had filed the photos in the order of the years the trips were taken. As I opened the cover my eyes gazed upon remembrances of the trip Kathleen and I had taken to Italy. It seemed like just yesterday we were landing at the Venice airport. Our trip had taken us through JFK airport in New York and on to the Frankfurt airport in Germany and finally our destination in Venice. After all my years of waiting I was finally there.

We boarded the water taxi near the airport and crossed the canal to our hotel. Seeing Venice from the water was amazing. We passed by St. Mark's Square, which included the Doge's Palace and the clock tower, before reaching our destination. We took our luggage to our room, and even though we had been traveling all night and were tired, the urge to walk across the bridges and through the streets of Venice was irresistible.

We were getting hungry so we decided to stop at a small local trattoria for lunch. On the way Kathleen spotted a local vendor selling purses. She saw one she liked and just had to buy it. We were in Venice for less than an hour and a purse was being purchased. You had to love her, I thought, as I continued to look at the pictures. I thought of the glass factory tour in Murano. I eyed the one photo that was taken by a group member that showed Kathleen and me sitting in the factory watching a demonstration. She was smiling, as she almost always did. It was very emotional. I continued through the photos of our trip.

We made stops in Pisa, Florence, Assisi, and finally Rome. There were pictures from all the locations. The stop in Pisa was cold and snowy, and after everyone saw the cathedral, baptistery, and leaning tower, the most popular spot was a coffee shop. Everyone crowded in to get a hot cup of coffee and to warm up. Our stop at Pisa was brief and we reloaded on the bus and set route for Florence. The snow continued and in the mountains it became worse. There was an accident on the highway that brought all traffic to a stop. We sat on the bus not moving for over an hour, and I remembered the snow seemed to get heavier. I remember thinking I hope we make it to Florence safely. We were two hours late, but finally made it to Firenze, as they say in Italy.

Seeing the setting, including the Ponte Vecchio with all its jewelry, the Academia with the statue of David, and the clothing and gold shops, was exciting. My mind went to the bus ride around the area and standing at a scenic overlook on the side of the Arno River across from the city. It was here that Kathleen and I took a picture with the city of Florence in the background. Every time I looked at it, framed next to a small piece of art purchased at that stop, I had a difficult time controlling my emotions. Florence was great.

Our next stop was Assisi. We climbed the hill to visit the cathedral that was built in honor of St. Francis of Assisi. The building was a beautiful structure containing much artwork on the walls and architecture that would be difficult to match today.

Turning the page in the album, I was looking at the photographs from Rome, the Eternal City. I could not take in the sites fast enough. The Coliseum, the Forum, and the many churches headlined by St. Peter's Basilica in Vatican City, which is not in Rome, but is in very close proximity.

I gazed at the pictures taken in the Vatican Museum, the Sistine Chapel, and finally St. Peter's Cathedral. I remembered walking in the huge building and the first piece of art I saw was the sculpture Pieta by Michelangelo, the work showing the Blessed Mother holding the body of her son Jesus. It was magnificent.

There were many side altars surrounding the inside of the structure, but to see the main altar where only the Pope offered Mass was thrilling. I thought while looking at the photos how I'd stood at the entrance to St. Peter's and walked the entire length of the main aisle and did not stop until I could go no closer to the main altar. I looked up, the domed ceiling with all its artwork. It was beyond words. My only regret was that our stay was not longer to allow Kathleen and me to take in more of the main cathedral of all the Roman Catholics of the world. I always said if I ever was to marry again it would be in the Vatican.

I continued through the album and the pictures of Italy came to an end. The last photograph was of Kathleen and me standing with the opera singers that performed for us at a special dinner show on our last night. The sites and activities in the cities of Italy were great, but holding hands with Kathleen while walking the streets was the highlight that would stay with me forever. I took a breath after replaying this marvelous journey.

As I turned the page, memories of a new journey were beginning. On this trip I was excited to have with me the new love in my life, Jane Ivan. Jane was reluctant to go, for she was not fond of flying over seven hours across the ocean; it made her very nervous. We took off for Paris from JFK airport, which had been the departing site for the trip to Italy. I was thinking of Jane telling me later how she'd seriously considered going back to Pittsburgh because of her fears. I was glad that she'd stayed. The trip was very memorable.

I remembered we'd landed at Charles de Gaulle Airport and then were transported to our hotel. There were other visitors in the van. Their hotels were in different parts of the city. The van passed by many of the major landmarks of the city: the Eiffel Tower, the Arc de Triomphe, and we even drove down the Champs-Elysees to the Seine River, from which we could see Notre Dame. We had been in Paris only a short time, but we'd already had the pleasure of seeing different neighborhoods as well as some of the notable sites. Our visit was displayed by the pictures in the album, Jane and me at the Eiffel Tower and the Arc de Triomphe, just to mention two.

Our two days in Paris went quickly. We were able to go to the Louvre and see the Mona Lisa. There Jane took my picture with one of the most famous pieces of art in history over my left shoulder. Jane was a great photographer, tolerating my continued desire to take pictures at various spots around the city.

As our stay ended in Paris we continued our trip, riding the train to Avignon. The European rail system is great and the views from the car were wonderful. The album contents included our tour through the cathedral in Avignon, which for about sixty eight years was the home of the Pope because of uprisings between the papacy and the French crown. Seven popes resided in Avignon during this period.

My thoughts went to us having dinner at a small restaurant in Avignon. I remembered it as Lou Mistral. Jane ordered a chicken dish and I had a sausage-and-bean plate. As I replayed this journey I couldn't help remembering Jane's reaction to how delicious her dish was and how many times since then we had talked about that dinner.

I continued through the album, which showed our next stop, Cannes, for lunch. Jane and I walked along the beach of the Mediterranean and opted to eat at a restaurant right on the water. As I looked at the picture of my meal choice, a Nicoise salad, I could almost taste it. I think the fact that the day was beautiful with warm sunshine, and being right on the water, made the dish taste even better. As I thought back it was my favorite meal.

I thought of us loading back on the bus and arriving at our hotel in Nice. I remember holding Jane's hand and walking on the Promenade des Anglais while looking at the beachgoers sunbathing on a rock-covered Nice beach. I thought of my first venture to the beach and seeing the reality that French ladies did go topless at the beach. I had to be honest: there were times when the perception was better than the reality.

I remembered going to the Hotel Negresco, a favorite hotel on the French Riviera, and having their signature drink, a Negroni: sweet red vermouth, Campari, and gin, garnished with an orange peel. Jane opted only to have a taste of mine. As I remember, it was good that she refrained because I had a difficult time walking back outside after finishing my order.

The album pages went on to show our side trip to the Principality of Monaco and our evening in Monte Carlo. We dressed more formally, and Jane looked beautiful in her black dress and jewelry that she selected. I found a seat at a blackjack table in the Grand Casino while Jane bided her time playing the slot machines. I kept an eye out for her and watched as she nervously crossed the floor of the casino. She kept looking for me. I was able to get her attention from my seat as the dealer continued to pass out the cards. Jane came over.

"Jake, I was worried. I did not know where you were and I did not know what to do."

I replied, "I knew where you were. You know I would never let anything happen to you."

I had won about a hundred and fifty euro at the blackjack table in the short period I'd played. As we walked away from the table I spotted a roulette wheel. I asked Jane to give me a number and I was going to put twenty-five Euros from my winnings on that number. A win would net us eight hundred seventy-five Euros.

Jane selected seventeen. The wheel spun and the white ball circled in the trough. The ball fell and landed on the seventeen. Our twenty-five Euros had become eight hundred seventy-five Euros. Jane had yet to realize that had happened.

The dealer voiced, "Seventeen." It was then Jane realized that was our number and that we had won.

The dealer started paying us our winnings. Jane's eyes lit up like stars as the chips were set in front of us.

"How much did we win?" she asked.

I responded in her ear, "Over a thousand U.S. dollars, considering the exchange rate."

I would treasure that look on her face forever. The twenty-five euro chips that were on the winning number I gave to the dealer. "Merci, monsieur," he replied with a smile.

It was time for Jane and me to celebrate. We exited the casino and went to the Hotel de Paris for their specialty drink, a martini. Our drinks were especially good, being as they were paid for by the winnings. After finishing our drinks we left the hotel, which was just across the street from the Grand Casino. I thought about the beautiful cars that were parked in front. There were Ferraris, Bentleys, Rolls-Royces, and the like. Those people in Monaco knew how to live.

CHAPTER 19
THE HELP

A KNOCK ON THE DOOR startled me out of my pictorial-journey trance. I opened the door to see the smiling face of Luke Turkal. He had already opened the storm door and entered once the metal front door was opened.

"How you doing, buddy?" Luke inquired.

"You know me, Luke, always living the dream. What is going on?"

"Well, Natasha is out shopping for the day and I thought you might want to go out for dinner. What say we go up to the City Line Diner?" This was a local restaurant very near to my house.

Luke continued, "I know it is dinnertime, or at least close, but they serve breakfast all day so we could have breakfast for dinner. You know we both like the home fries they make. We can team them up with some sausage and eggs and rye toast and wash it all down with a fresh cup of coffee."

I thought for a minute and decided why not. I still had the photo album in my hand. Luke noticed and asked, "Reminiscing about your trips?"

"Yes. Every now and then I pull out the pictures. These are my souvenirs. The memories of being with Kathleen in Italy and being with Jane on later trips are the best."

Luke said he would drive the short distance to the diner. We did not even warm the seats of the car and we were there. The City Line seemed to have been there forever. As we entered the door we viewed the counter on the right with the red-capped stools. There was a row of tables down the middle of the floor and booths hugging the windows on the left. The two amigos took the booth in the rear of the room. It was not long before the waitress approached the booth.

"Do you guys need menus?"

Luke replied, "No. We are going to have breakfast for dinner."

With that he placed the order for both of us, just as he'd rehearsed it. Eggs over medium, sausage, home fries, and rye toast, with coffee to drink.

"You got it, sweetie," our server replied.

The girls here made a habit of using "sweetie," "honey," "sugar," or some other friendly moniker.

While we were waiting for our food, Luke and I started talking about helping out our fellow man. Luke was a very generous person and if he felt it proper he would, as the expression went, "Give them the shirt off his back."

While chatting, Luke told me a story I had heard many times before, and I listened again. He recalled a Sunday before church services when, while he was outside the building, a homeless man approached him. Luke asked him if there was anything he could do for him. The man only had the clothes on his back and not much more. Luke's church had a clothing room that took in usable garments and made them available to the needy. He took the man into the room and outfitted him with good-looking clothes that fit pretty well. He even found him a pair of shoes that were his size. The only clothing that he did not have was socks. This said, Luke took off the socks he was wearing and gave them to the man in need.

They then proceeded to go into the church and have the pastor and other members of the congregation take off their socks so that they could give them to him as well. This was probably the first and only time the reverend stood at the pulpit and performed his Sunday service in his vestments and no socks, thanks to the goodness of Luke. Luke even assisted the man financially by giving him some cash. Needless to say, the man was very happy. He thanked Luke for his generosity and was on his way. To my knowledge, he never saw him again. I never get tired of listening to this story, and Luke is proud to continue to tell it. The part about the socks always brings a grin to his face.

Our food arrived and we continued to talk about helping the homeless. "You know, my brother," I voiced to Luke, "I have been thinking about an idea for a while. There are approximately three thousand counties in this country, and surveys show there are one point five million homeless people.

"If each county made an effort to take in, find housing and work for five hundred people, a lot of the problem could be corrected. Now this is an average, but the bigger counties could take in more and the smaller ones less. A system could be set up where the homeless could come in and register for the program through local agencies. Those able-bodied individuals could get minimum wage or slightly higher jobs to pay their expenses and would have to comply with the rules established for the program. If they do not work or take care of their living quarters they unfortunately would end up where they came from. The choice would be up to the individuals.

"I know that there are a percentage of homeless that will not accept or comply with the program, but if some are helped it would be a win. It may not remedy every situation, but it could put a dent in the problem. I know it looks to be a complicated problem, but as Dr. Seuss says, 'Complicated problems can be solved by simple solutions.'"

Luke took my "ism" in and said maybe if the idea got to the right people it could work. He suggested running the idea past the minister at his church. He felt that if all of the churches of his faith felt the program was doable it would be a good start. The hope would be other religious groups would join in across the country and with the help of some media coverage maybe some of the elected officials in the state and federal positions would join the effort.

Luke, being the generous helping person that he was, started to get excited about the idea.

"Jake, you're always thinking. This idea or "ism" as you call it could go somewhere. Let's work on it."

"I'll help where I can, Luke. It is a big undertaking, but you know the expression, 'Every journey starts with the first step.'"

We finished our breakfast for dinner and were getting ready to exit the booth to pay our bill. I told Luke to sit tight, as I had to use the restroom. As I exited the men's room I could see Luke sitting in the booth, and he was giving me a strange eye and hand gestures. I hesitated, as a partition blocked me from the view of the rest of the diner. I heard a voice.

"Just give me the money in the register and nobody gets hurt."

I peeked carefully around the wall and saw a guy standing at the counter with his hand in his coat pocket, which the waitress took to be a gun. There was a coat rack near the area where I was standing and on it hung a metal cane that belonged to one of the other customers. I showed the cane to Luke and gestured to him to be ready.

The thief was only a short distance from my position. I pondered the situation quickly and, as bad a decision as it might have been, I burst out from behind the wall and smacked the cane across the head of the robber. The customers in the diner reacted with screams and yells. He dropped immediately and Luke and I were on him before he hit the ground. His hand exited his pocket which, thank goodness, only held a hairbrush, not a handgun. He was not a big guy and we were able to put him down, and with the help of the fix-all tool, duct tape, we were able to bind his hands and feet as we waited for the police. The cane to the head had really stunned the guy and he had a lump on his head to prove it.

The Follansville police arrived quickly and the criminal was taken into custody. The backup police officers asked some questions to get the details as to what happened. The waitress was still rattled, so when the officer who we knew approached Luke and me, we told him that in the guy's haste to get away he tripped over a chair and fell and hit his head on the table, enabling us to apprehend him. The cane had already been returned to its original position on the coat rack.

Luke spoke. "That's what happened, Officer. He was just in too much of a hurry. Luckily, he did not have a gun and nobody was hurt."

The officer stared at us with the look of "Sounds a little fishy to me, but I will go with it." With that, Luke and I patted the officer on the back and complimented him and the rest of the department on the fine job they did.

Luke suggested jokingly, "Since we have police protection we should leave with the officer so we could be guaranteed safety to the car."

As we started our short ride back to my house I asked Luke if he was available to give me a lift to the airport for my trip to Florida. I was leaving on Saturday morning and he would be doing me a big favor if he was able to get me there. Luke said he would. I told him I would call him and give him the time of the required pickup. We shook hands and I walked toward my home as he drove away.

The time was getting close to seven o'clock and I quickly entered the house and positioned myself in the recliner to watch Jeopardy. At my age I don't even buy green bananas anymore. I have to work to keep the mind and body in shape to hopefully have a longer, healthier life. I always refer to my lifeline, the crease in the hand that runs from the middle of your palm on the index finger side and arcs around the thumb. Mine is very long and definitive, but as I always say, I do not know where I am on the line. Hopefully God will bless me and allow me to live many more years with a strong mind and body, but that's God's decision, not mine.

John Mihalyo

CHAPTER 20
THE BEACH

SATURDAY CAME QUICKLY, AND MY journey to Florida was about to begin. I asked Luke to pick me up at ten a.m. My flight was nonstop and was scheduled to leave at noon. Luke arrived promptly at the hour, and after our greetings and loading the suitcases and golf clubs in the car, we were on our way. The trip to the airport was less than half an hour. Luke and I had a general conversation, and before we knew it we were at the airport. There was no need him for him to park the car in a lot. He merely pulled up to the terminal for the airline and I unloaded my suitcase and clubs, along with a carry-on. We bid each other goodbye with a hug. The stop was short. This was usually the case because the state troopers patrolled the area and did not let one linger either to pick up or drop off passengers.

The skycap checked my luggage. I made my way to the gate, going through the TSA security en route. The lines were not very long, and being that I had TSA PreCheck, I was able to get through very quickly.

The flight left right on time, and in a little over two hours I arrived at the Tampa International Airport. I retrieved my bags and exited the door to wait for my driver to take me to my residence. My cell phone rang.

The voice on the other end after my "Hello" spoke. "This is Larry, your driver. Where are you located?"

I informed him of my location, and he responded that he would pick me up in ten minutes as scheduled.

The vehicle left the airport and followed the signs for I-275 to St. Petersburg. It was a beautiful day, and as we drove south I was able to see the water of Tampa Bay on both sides of the freeway. It was a delightful sight. I remember saying to myself, "I'm home."

Larry and I talked along the way. The conversation was: "How was the weather? Has there been any rain? What is the forecast for the week?" Just routine information for someone just arriving.

We were lucky that once exiting the interstate we did not catch many red lights. If you just miss a green light you can end up waiting for a while for the next one, depending on the intersection. I always said, when God gave out patience he missed me completely. There are days when I am driving that it seems like I catch every red light. I just think I am being tested.

We arrived at my dwelling and unloaded my bags. My ride had been paid for in advance, so I only had to tip Larry and he was gone. I unlocked the door and entered "heaven," as I called it. The entire place was painted white with white tile floors, and with the sun beaming through the windows, it reminded me of movies depicting heaven. The robes are white, the clouds are white and everyone in the shot is glowing white. I thought to myself, if heaven is this good I look forward to getting there, but not right away. I hope the good Lord will allow me many more years of living in heaven on earth, as I always say, "living the dream."

I unpacked my bags, which consisted of mainly underwear, shorts, T-shirts, and sneakers. I had left clothes and other items from my previous stays, so there was not a need to bring much from up north. The balance of the day was spent checking on the property and relaxing. Dinner time approached. Being retired, dinner hour has no set time. I do not wear a watch, so when I am hungry I eat, when I am tired I go to sleep, and when I feel rested I get up. The sun being out means it's daytime, and when darkness falls it is nighttime. If I have to know the time, I look at my cell phone.

My Cadillac turned right over. It had not been driven much, but my neighbor Ron had been starting it up periodically to keep the battery charged. Thus far, all was good. I headed out to dinner, and on the way back stopped for a few groceries. Tomorrow off to the beach.

I rolled out of my king-sized bed at eight a.m. to start my day. After offering thanks to the Lord for all of my blessings I started my morning routine. I performed my bathroom ritual and headed to the kitchen. The next order of business was a cup of coffee with milk, no sugar. I do not use sugar in anything, but a cookie or piece of lemon loaf or some sweet was almost always part of the wake-up process.

I turned on the television to watch the national news to see what was happening in the world. The news was the usual: The Democrats disagree with the Republicans and the Republicans object to the Democrats. The American people who elected these individuals to represent them are left hanging. Someday, and that day will probably never come, I would love to see a politician stand in front of a television camera and say, "I am voting for or against a substantial bill because it is the right thing for the American people. I know my fellow party members do not agree with me, but in my heart I have to do it. This said, if the vote causes me to not get re-elected, so be it; I will go back to my state with a clear conscience when my term ends."

Would such an action be a shocker? The last time and maybe the only time in recent years I saw both parties get together on anything was when they sang "God Bless America" in front of the Capitol after the 9/11 tragedy. I really hope we do not have to have another event of this magnitude to get both parties to agree.

The day was going to be a typical Florida day, clear skies and sunshine with temperatures in the high seventies or low eighties with a light breeze. A great beach day was shaping up. I put on my bathing suit, packed up a towel, suntan lotion, a bottle of water, donned my sunglasses and hat and took the Cadillac for a little exercise by driving to the beach. The beach was only a short distance from my living quarters, and if I did not hit many red lights, ten to fifteen minutes would be my traveling time.

My estimates were correct, and luckily I found a parking space right near a public access point to the beach. I grabbed my packed beach bag and unloaded the beach chair out of the trunk. The walk to the beach was only a couple hundred yards. The path took me down a side street over a wooden walkway and onto the white-sand beach. I set up my chair and sat down to enjoy the view. The sky seemed to be bluer than when I left home, and the smell of the salt water and the mild breeze made for a good start to the beach visit. The waves were not very high, and with the sun shining down on the small caps, the water appeared to be full of diamonds.

The noon hour had not arrived, but many beach goers, with their multi-colored umbrellas, beach chairs, and towels, had already secured their spots. There was a continual parade of walkers and joggers going up and down the hard-sand area, ladies in bikinis, two-piece and one-piece bathing suits of many colors, as well as men in their swimsuits of various lengths, with an occasional Speedo design in the mix. As I looked north and south from my location, I could see piers extending out into the water. These structures were popular spots for folks to fish and try to land the night's dinner. I asked a guy fishing there one day if he was having any luck. He said no, because if he caught it he would have to clean it. He probably was not even using a hook, just enjoying the day.

As I sat in my chair, I became hypnotized by the constant roar of the water. As I looked across the Gulf of Mexico, my memory took me thousands of miles to the west to the Hawaiian Islands. I was very fortunate in my younger years, after graduating from college, to work for in the government aka. The United States Army. When my tour of duty ended I was invited by a friend in my outfit to visit him in Hawaii. How could I refuse? This had been a dream of mine since I was a kid. I can remember getting up for school in the morning. The black and white television was usually tuned into the Today Show hosted by Dave Garroway and his partner Jack Lescoulie. Every day the show would roll the forecasted high temperatures on screen of cities around the United States. I always paid particular attention to Honolulu and always dreamed that I would visit there someday. Thanks to my friend Rob Banner, my dream was becoming a reality. Rob was a great guy and a good soldier. He was a medic in our unit. A lot of the guys referred to him as Doc Banner. Rob was still an active member of the Army stationed at Schofield Barracks on the island of Oahu. This allowed me to accompany him around the post and utilize the facilities.

The island was beautiful, and the weather was almost always perfect. It was definitely paradise in the Pacific. While visiting Rob on the island, I remember deciding to get certified as a scuba diver. The program was offered at Schofield Barracks. They had an Olympic-sized pool at the post where the diving instructions would be held. I remember thinking; this will be great; how hard could it be? I would put on the air tank, mask, and fins, and away I would go. Boy was I wrong.

My first clue should have been meeting our instructor, Victor Fury, a retired Marine, who in his active duty days, was known as Drill Sergeant Victor Fury. The guys in the class called him the Mad Hungarian. He was tough. The session was not a float down the lazy river.

Sergeant Fury, as I found out, had experienced some very difficult times during his years in the Corps. He persevered and managed to end his career as a drill sergeant. He was now retired and had started a second career as a teacher. He was very easy going. He kept himself in very good physical condition. He would emphasize to us during every class to pay attention to him and remember every little detail, one day it could save our life. He was a very experienced expert certified diver who helped tie the transatlantic cable. He knew what he was talking about.

John Mihalyo

The first hour of training was spent going through the manual that was selected for the class. The next hour and a half to two hours was spent in the pool. We put on our equipment and started swimming laps around the pool using a snorkel. There were assistants in the pool making sure you swam around the pool and did not take short cuts. These fellows were even nice enough to pull your mask off once in a while. This warm up, as the sarge called it, lasted for about fifteen to twenty minutes. We were then instructed to line up in the pool on one end and had to swim down and back. After each trip, make an adjustment to your gear; take your tank off, down and back; put your tank on, down and back; take your weight belt off, down and back; put the weight belt on, down and back. After about an hour of this I thought, this is supposed to be fun, not Navy Seal training.

The gentle pace of the waves on the Gulf beach helped me to continue thinking about Hawaii. After weeks of training in the pool, the class was ready for our certification dive in the ocean. I remember walking out on a coral reef about ten feet above the Pacific Ocean. I had all my equipment in my hands: tank, mask, snorkel, fins, weight belt, and life jacket, or Mae West as it was commonly called. The task was to jump into the water that was crashing off the rocks and coral and put all of the equipment on. Once this was completed, the class was taken out so we could get the feel of swimming into

122

a current known as the Honolulu Express. I would be swimming in one direction and the current was taking me backward, up and down with the waves, while salt water was going down my snorkel. It did not take long before everybody's breakfast became part of the ocean. There was still fun to be had.

It was time to practice coming out of the water by climbing up the coral cliffs with all the equipment. The trick was to ride the waves and grab hold of the coral formation and climb out of the water. I kept thinking, there is a nice sandy beach a short distance away – why not just exit there? The sarge expressed the fact that you would not always have such an easy exit, and it was necessary to learn the technique of landing on the cliffs.

So as I remember it, I was seasick. I was bleeding from the cuts from the coral, and now it was time to go down under the surface sixty to eighty feet in nice warm water. My mind went to, aren't sharks drawn by blood? As I descended below the surface I kept thinking, I hope the sharks are a long way off.

I reached the bottom of the ocean, and the first order of business was to take off my mask and to put it back on, using the technique we were taught to clear the mask of water. I was able to complete that task successfully. The last and most questionable task remained. I had to stay on the bottom and run my air tank out of air. The theory was that even though you had little or no air at sixty-plus feet, as you ascended at one foot per second there would be air in the tank. So I sat and watched the tropical fish swim by my mask as I waited until the sarge saw that my tank gauge measured "E." I was then released to ascend. The fact that I was spending this beautiful day on the Gulf of Mexico proved that I survived.

CHAPTER *21*
THE REMEMBRANCE

I SNAPPED OUT OF MY trance of my time in Hawaii at the sound of seagulls squawking near me, hoping to find a morsel or more of food to eat. They found nothing and took off to their next prey. There were some children playing on the beach, and I thought of my grandchildren: James, Grace, Lucy, Rose, and Jack, and how much fun they would have here. They could ride some waves, build sandcastles, and look for the perfect shell. There is no better place for children to have fun than a day at the beach.

As I sat enjoying my surroundings I started thinking. In this day and age the average person lives to be around seventy-eight years old, some a little longer and unfortunately some do not make the number. That means the average person has about twenty-eight thousand mornings in his or her life. As with most of us, the majority of these mornings or days are spent getting up and going to work. We go out to our place of employment, such as Follansville Steel, to earn a living to put bread on the table and keep a roof over the head of our families. I thank God every day for allowing me to spend my remaining days on this earth doing what I enjoy and not having to work. For those who say, "I like my job. I do not mind working," I say to them, "Keep working, because if you like what you're doing then it is not work."

When you spend a day at the beach alone, you have a lot of time to think about things that happened in your life. A person does not realize how many memories are stored up in their brain. The surroundings bring back many thoughts. Some are happy and some are sad. There are those that bring a grin and those that bring a tear. As I sat on my chair, a little girl with strawberry-red hair appeared. She was doing what most children do at water's edge and she really seemed to be enjoying her day. Watching this pretty young girl took me back to an evening I spent with my mother shortly before she passed away.

Hilda Virginia Regina Bono Million, as she would proudly brag, was born to an Italian father and mother in Follansville. She spent almost her entire life living in the small town. Even after getting married to my father at the young age of twenty, only a couple years of her life were spent outside the town of her birth. Mom loved life. She always smiled and was always there when someone needed help. This particular night I visited her and, as was our norm, we watched the game shows on television. Wheel of Fortune was one of her favorites, and we would play against each other to see who would solve the puzzle first. Suddenly, as Mom was reclining on the couch, she pointed to the end of the sofa and said to me, "Do you see that little girl?"

This comment caught me by surprise and I went along with the question. The inquiry continued.

"Right there at the end of the sofa. She has strawberry-red curly hair. Isn't she cute?" Mom stated. She briefly turned her head to get more comfortable. As she looked back she became sad. "Oh, she left. You did see her, didn't you, Jake?"

"Sorry, Mom, I missed her. I guess I did not look quick enough. You know these youngsters; they go in and out pretty fast."

My mother was still of sound mind, so my feeling is she saw an angel who was preparing the way for her to leave for heaven. It was not long after this experience that this beautiful woman left this earth to take her place among the believers who ask God to allow them a place next to him.

I glanced up to the heavens and with a tear in my eye. The words crossed my lips, "I love you, Mom."

As these words crossed my lips, I wished that I would have used the expression more than I did while all those who did so much for me were still alive. Just three little words, "I love you," can make such a difference. We take for granted that before people die they will get older, become ill, and gradually pass away, so until that time comes there is no rush to show your feelings and tell them you love them.

As I stared out into the Gulf, I saw a cruise ship out in the distance. My mind began to reminisce again. I thought of my dad, John Million. He was a hard-working dedicated employee of the steel plant. He was not formally educated, but I always said he went to the school that taught everything. He could do any job that he set his mind to doing. Electrical work, carpentry, plumbing, mechanical work – you name it, he could do it.

I remember asking him one day about doing a big repair job to our family car. I asked if he was sure he could handle it. He replied, "It is broke when I'm starting." The joke was he did the repairs, had parts left over, and the car ran fine.

Dad worked hard his entire life and finally decided to retire. He called Mom one day and asked her if she wanted to go on a cruise. Mom was all for it, so he made the arrangements. They went on the cruise, and when they returned home we talked on the phone. I remember Mom saying what a joy Dad was on the trip and what a great time they had. Then Dad took the phone and proceeded to tell me how great the trip was and how he got to visit the engine room of the ship. He was describing the machines that allowed the ship to function. I closed our conversation by saying we would be down for a visit tomorrow and he could tell me more about his journey.

I never was able to hear more about the trip. I received the call the next day saying that my dad, at a very young age in today's world, had passed away. There were no more chances to say, "I love you, Dad." I looked at the cruise ship, remembering my dad.

Matthew chapter 24, verse 36 of the Bible reads: "No one knows, however, when that day and hour will come." Verse 44 reads: "So then you also must always be ready because the Son of Man will come at an hour when you are not expecting him."

With these passages in mind, and since none of us know our date to leave this earth, the thought crossed my mind, you can do little for those you love when they are gone, but you can do so much when they are still with you.

I had been on the beach for a couple of hours, and since I was just starting to work on a tan I decided I'd had enough sun for the day. I would have plenty of opportunities since I was planning on being in Florida at least until the cold weather in the north ended.

John Mihalyo

CHAPTER 22
THE MEETING

I ARRIVED BACK AT HOME and was preparing to fix myself some lunch as my phone rang. It was Terry Day.

"Hey, horse trader, how's the weather down there?"

I replied, "The weather is great. I am just living the dream. How are things in your neck of the woods?"

Terry voiced back, "Things are good. It is a beautiful fall day. The reason for the call is that I was looking at the racing form for today and there are a couple of picks I like, and if you could use a few extra dollars you might want to make a wager."

Terry did not call often, but when he did I knew he really liked his selections. He gave me his choices and then said he had a funny story to tell me.

Terry stated, "You know Malocchio, don't you?" he asked.

"Who doesn't?" I replied. "Anyone who goes to the track knows Malocchio. He is bad luck waiting to happen."

Malocchio is the Italian word for "Evil Eye" or "Bad Luck." If Malocchio bet your horse, your chances of winning were two, slim and none. He was a black cat, broken mirror, and walking under a ladder all in one.

Terry continued. "Well, the other day he caused quite a ruckus in the men's room. There was a guy in a stall, and Malocchio was beating on the door, telling him to get out, because he was in his stall, and he had to use it before the races started or he would have bad luck. He was yelling quite loudly, and finally security had to come in and escort him out. As the story goes, Malocchio had a winner the other day, probably his first in eons, and because he used the stall that day he felt it gave him good luck. Is that a hoot or what?" Terry asked.

I listened to Terry's story and could not believe what I was hearing. "I have heard of guys having lucky hats, lucky socks, and even not washing their underwear, and wearing the same outfit again after a winning day, but the toilet stall story takes all."

Terry and I both laughed about the story. I thanked him for calling with the picks. "Let's hope you're hot today, Ter. You are the best handicapper I know."

Terry responded, "Let's bring them in. We will talk later."

I was able to make the bets on my online betting site. The wagers were not big, but some of Terry's picks had some good odds, so if they came in I would make a little extra spending money.

I had to get moving and go to the grocery store. When I arrived I picked up the basics: milk, bread, eggs, and the like, but I had to restock the shelves and refrigerator since I was going to be in Florida for the snowy cold season of the north. This most likely meant not returning back to Follansville until April.

I parked the car in the market lot and grabbed a basket left by patrons who, for whatever the reason, left them in one of the stalls so no one could park there. I just wonder about their reasoning. I think sometimes laziness or being inconsiderate. I like to think that the person was not physically able to return the basket to the designated return area.

Once in the store, I was parading up and down the aisles and filling my basket with essentials and impulse items. I guess the theory to never shop on an empty stomach may have some merit. I was getting hungry. As I made a turn at the end of an aisle to head up the next one, I heard a voice. "Jake, Jake Million, how the heck are you?"

It was Thomas Parker, a fellow that I had worked with in the plant years back. He had retired and moved to Florida. Thomas was a good worker, the kind of guy you did not have to tell what to do. He knew his job and he did it well.

Thomas had relocated to Follansville from the Pittsburgh area. He had attended Westinghouse High School, an inner-city school. The records show that Thomas was an excellent athlete. He was a star in multiple sports – in football, basketball, and baseball –

earning all-state honors in all three. He even ran track when he was available, participating in the one-hundred- and two-hundred-yard dash, as well as the sprint relays. Those that knew Thomas in his younger days say he was the best around.

We chatted briefly and agreed to meet at the coffee shop in the store. Once there, we talked about some of the guys who we worked with. Some had passed away, while others were alive and well; there were a few who were still working. Thomas was in the department when I was a young buck just out of the management training program. I was assigned to a department, and I must admit was not happy. The area I was assigned to was an older operation that I felt would be shutting down in a few years due to the more modern facilities that had been put in operation.

"You know, Jake," Thomas recalled, "it seems to me that you moved up the ladder pretty quickly. You went from go-for" - or gopher as we called it - "to yard foreman to mill foreman to general foreman in what seemed to be no time."

"You're right, Thomas. As I think back, it was only a few years. Getting that general foreman position was a big surprise. You may remember Thaddeus Kent had the job, and Simon Murdock was his understudy."

I continued, "Here's where the story gets interesting. One day my wife, Kathleen, and her friend decided to go to a card reader. They were interested in her telling them what was going to happen in their lives. I could not believe she was going to see this lady, but if that's what she wanted to do and it made her happy, that's what counted. When she returned home I asked what the card reader told her. The reader did not tell negative things, only positive outlooks that she saw in Kathleen's life, as well as her loved ones. I cannot remember the things she told me that were going to happen in her life, but I remember what she said was going to happen to me. The reader told her that I was going to get a promotion and become general foreman. I saw no way this was going to happen. Thaddeus Kent was an experienced man of steel and was doing fine in the job. If anything happened to him, I could see where Simon Murdock would take over. It seemed only right. Do you agree, Thomas?"

He nodded as I continued. "Kathleen said, 'That's what she told me. We will see.'"

"Surprisingly, Thaddeus Kent had a heart attack and had to retire. Simon Murdock saw to it that his duties were performed on a temporary basis. It was not long after Thaddeus's medical misfortune that I was called to the superintendent's office. He informed me that he wanted me to take over the general foreman's position. I arrived home that night and told Kathleen the news. She gave me a look as if to say, I told you so. Then it hit me, the card reader's predictions. That's the story, Thomas.

Kathleen never went back to the reader. I can't say if any of her predictions came true, but mine sure did."

Thomas listened to my story and just shook his head. Then he spoke. "I have no doubt that it worked out well for everyone. The guys liked you. You treated them with respect. When they needed told about something, you did it in a professional manner and kept the comments constructive, not destructive."

"That was my goal, Thomas. Even when I became superintendent and then manager I tried to treat the workers fairly. I know that some decisions were not always favorable with everyone, but I tried to base my decisions on what was best for the company. Hopefully the effects on the men were minimal. Like I always said, their job was to make me look good. I tried to return the favor by treating them as fair as possible."

Thomas and I talked a while longer, with him telling me about his life since he retired. He talked about his family and, as most grandfathers are, he was proud of his grandchildren. We shook hands and agreed to stay in touch whenever possible. With that said, I hurried home to get the items that needed to be refrigerated put away.

CHAPTER 23
THE ROUND

THE DAYS OF ENJOYING THE warm Florida sunshine went by quickly. Easter was getting near on the calendar, so I scheduled my flight back home to be there for the holiday. I started preparing my Florida home for departure, cleaning out any food items that would not keep, and only keeping what I would use in my remaining days.

The day came for departure, and I had contacted Larry my driver to pick me up so that I would have plenty of time to make my flight. My last duties were to take out the trash, secure all of the windows, set the thermostat at the proper temperature, and turn off the water. I completed all of my duties, and as scheduled, Larry arrived to transport me to the airport.

"How was your stay, Jake?" Larry asked.

"Very nice, Larry. The weather was good. Jane was able to visit for awhile. We had some great meals, we played some golf, and we went to the horse track just about every week, where I was able to hold my own. I managed to withdraw more than I deposited at the bank. My time here in Florida seemed to fly by."

Larry knew what I was referring to. "I know," he said, "You never lose. You've told me you call it a bank. Sometimes you deposit and other times you withdraw."

We arrived at the airport. Larry helped me unload my bags. I bid him farewell and had the skycap check my bags. The only thing left to do now was go through security and wait for the flight to depart.

All went smooth. The lines at security were not that long, and I was able to make it through fairly quickly. I took a seat at my gate area and passed the time doing what most do, people watching. I saw men and women dressed very professionally. Then there were others that looked like they just rolled out of bed, splashed water on their face, put on their cleanest dirty shirt or jeans, and headed to the airport. I was most amazed by the amount of carry-on luggage people brought.

The airlines allow you one piece of carry-on that must curtail to size specifications and one personal item. I watched people with carry-on luggage that was too big and a personal bag that was more like a second carry-on. Women had purses that were bigger than some of the bags they carried. Lest we forget the shopping bags of souvenirs and other miscellaneous items that were too valuable to check. The thought always crossed my mind, "Did you leave anything at home?"

The flight home was smooth and I arrived as scheduled. After securing my bags I walked outside of the terminal to the passenger pickup area, and as planned, there was Luke Turkal. As luck would have it, he arrived with perfect timing. I was going to call him on the cell phone to tell him I had arrived, but it was not necessary. He exited the car and we hugged and then loaded the bags.

"Your timing was perfect, Luke. I was just about to call you."

"I knew what time your flight arrived, so I assumed it was on time. I gave you some time to secure your bags and hoped that my estimates were good, and they were," Luke responded.

"I really appreciate you picking me up. Thank you."

We made small talk on the ride back, and before we knew it we arrived at my house. We unloaded the bags and bid each other adios. It was time for me to reestablish my residence in Follansville for now. I enjoyed my time in Florida and was giving serious consideration to selling my house and moving there permanently. I thought about getting in contact with a realtor to get some idea of the value of my home, as well as liquidating the contents. I pondered for awhile as I was unpacking and getting settled. I thought I have plenty of time to look into that possibility.

The next morning, I received a call from my son, John, who told me he had to come back to Follansville for a special education seminar that was being held at a nearby college. He asked if a round of golf could be arranged, as his seminar was only until noon on the final day, and he did not have to fly back home until late in the evening.

"I can handle that. I will get Mick Dehazi and Jas Readie to make up the foursome."

I arranged a tee time at the Pheasant Valley Golf Club. Mick and Jas were good guys to play with in a foursome. Mick was an older fraternity brother of John and I at State. He was a member when the fraternity was first founded. He was a good athlete in his day, playing on the college baseball team, and when he went into the Army, he played for a traveling team from the post. For his age, Mick played a good round of golf, and could beat a lot of guys much younger than him.

Jas was a real gentleman. He was very low key when he played, but a real good golfer. He had joined the over-seventy club age-wise, but it was not unusual for him to shoot par for eighteen holes, or close to it.

When the day of the match came, we all met on the first tee, and as luck would have it, we had clear sailing; there was no one in front of us. The first hole was an easy par five, and we were all able to reach the green in three and we all pared the hole with two putts. We were able to play at our own pace, and the round was going well. We were all playing pretty good golf with a lot of pars, a bogey here or there, and even a birdie on occasion.

We were all enjoying the round and each other's company as the sunshine began to fade. We arrived on the sixteenth hole, a downhill one hundred thirty-five-yard par three with a green that sloped strongly from right to left. The sun had gone down behind the trees so the green was shaded. We could follow the flight of the ball, but once it hit the green it was hard to see. We all hit our tee shots, with me hitting last.

"You know, guys," I said, "it has been a long time since I had a hole in one."

They all looked as if to say, when did you have a hole in one?

I quickly continued, "Over sixty years, and I am due."

They realized I had never had a hole in one. I teed up the ball and took a nice easy swing, and the ball sailed toward the right side of the green. It landed softly and started to roll down to the pin. Everybody got excited.

"Whoa," exclaimed John. "That is going to go in."

Jas chimed in. "Jake, I think this may be a first for you."

Mick exclaimed, "Nice shot, Jake," as the ball slowly rolled toward the hole. Then in the dusk of the evening, the ball disappeared. It was high fives and pandemonium. I was excited, my first hole in one. We took to our carts and headed for what we thought was a hole in one. As we neared the green, the excitement went away. My shot had stopped about one inch behind the hole, and because of the darkness of the area and the position of the pin we could not see the ball until we drew nearer to the green. I was disappointed and so were my playing companions.

My son, John, patted me on the back. "Great shot, Dad. I thought you had it."

Jas and Mick voiced similar compliments. I tapped in the one-inch putt for a birdie. My sixty-plus-year streak continued.

We finished the round, and John and I bid Mick and Jas farewell and headed back to my home. We freshened up and went out to JJ's for some ribs before he had to get back to the airport and fly home. We talked while we ate, mostly about sports. It was great to spend the day with John. The opportunities have become fewer and fewer since he relocated hours away from Follansville. I drove John to the airport and pulled up to the curbside drop-off for him to check his bags. We hugged and told each other that we loved one another. I asked John to text me that he arrived home safely. I looked back as he disappeared through the terminal doors. A tear came to my eye with the thought, "At my age, how many more times will we see each other?"

CHAPTER 24
THE ISM

THE NEXT DAY I AWOKE and performed my usual wake-up routine. As I had been away for a while, I decided to head downtown around the lunch hour to see what I had missed. The Mercedes turned over without a problem. I backed out of the garage. Since it was already a warm day, I put the top down and made my way to Bessie's. I parked in the lot outside the building. I looked over the vehicles that were occupying spaces prior to my arrival. There was a white van parked that I had no problem recognizing. It belonged to Phillip Hall, who was an electrician in town. On the side of the van were the words "Phillip Hall Electric. Let me remove your shorts."

Phillip had been in business for years, and he was a good man to hire for his type of work. Phillip was also a very religious person, whom I tried to avoid having a long conversation with because it usually ended in an extensive talk about some aspect of religion.

I entered the diner and was greeted warmly by Bessie. "Jake, you're back. You look great. I can see the weather was good. Nice tan."

"Thanks, Bessie. It is nice to be back."

I moved to occupy the booth in the rear, asking Bessie for a coffee as we separated. As I proceeded to the booth I spoke to the folks that were seated. Some I knew and some I did not, but as I have always said, it doesn't cost anything to be nice to people.

Phillip was one of those to whom I spoke, and it was not long before he made his way to where I was seated. Phillip greeted me with, "Praise the Lord, Jake. It is good to see you again."

I acknowledged. "Thank you, Phillip. It's good to see you as well."

Phillip started out the conversation casually, but it was not long before religion began to be a prominent part of the conversation. Phillip started talking about the bad people in the world. He continued on about how, if they did not change their ways, when they died they would be cast into the fires of hell.

He looked at me and said, "You believe that, don't you, Jake? You are a good Christian person. You read the Bible. The Bible tells us that's what is going to happen to sinners, right?"

I thought for a few second and decided to come back at Phillip with an "ism." "Phillip," I said, "how do you know that heaven and hell are not here on earth? Think about it."

I continued. "I am not saying people are reincarnated, but people die every day and babies are born every day.

Some are born in wonderful homes and are treated very well and enjoy a good healthy life. Then there are others who do not have it as good. They struggle making ends meet and have serious health problems. This is occurring not only in this country but around the world. People are being persecuted for their religious beliefs, they are lucky to have a roof over their heads to protect them from the sun and rain, they have little or no food. Could it be, Phillip, that these people were on this earth before and are now living in hell because of their previous lifestyle?"

I could see Phillip's mind working. I do not think anyone had ever proposed that scenario to him before.

I continued, "Phillip, have you ever talked to anyone who was in heaven? Do you really know what it is like there? Is it not possible that those who are living the good life here on earth are those who obeyed the Commandments and lived a good Christian life the first time around?"

I really had Phillip going now, to the point where he could not rebut. I had to back off.

"Phillip, I do not believe this and neither do you. I believe what the Bible says. God promises that we will be at his side in heaven if we live a good life. Those that do not will also have a chance to be at his side if they ask for forgiveness of their sins. I have not talked to anyone who has been to heaven, either, but I sure want to get there. I do not think any of us living today has any idea what it is going to be like in heaven. The most important thing is that all of us have to be ready when God calls. None of us know the hour or the day. I thank God for my blessings every day, and when he calls me, I want to be ready to go."

Phillip looked at me. "Jake," he said, "you had me going on that heaven and hell on earth thing." Phillip looked at his watch. "I have to get going, Jake. I have a few more jobs to do before the end of the day. Peace be with you, Jake, and may God watch over you and allow you to live many more healthy and prosperous years here on earth."

"Thank you, Phillip. I hope so."

CHAPTER 25
THE FINALE

"I HOPE SO, I HOPE SO, I hope so" kept echoing through my mind as I opened my eyes. The room was extremely quiet. The exception was an occasional beep from a piece of medical equipment or an announcement on the intercom paging a particular doctor. Room 711 was in the ICU unit, a private room, but it was far from empty. As I wiped my eyes to see clearer, sighs of relief came from all those who were next to me.

My eyes began to focus, and I saw Father Matthew standing next to me, holding his container of holy chrism. It seemed, as I was coming around, I could feel the light touch of his thumb or finger on my forehead. Next to him was Dr. Mark Capo, who had his stethoscope around his neck as he watched me become more alert. There were others.

As I turned my head slowly from side to side, I saw my son, John, and his wife, Theresa, as well as my daughter, Ann, with her husband, Jim. As I gazed further down the bed, I saw my brothers, Andrew and David, with their wives, Mary and Kathryn.

I started to move my head and I felt a hand curled up in a fist within my hand. It was Jane Ivan. This was a thing with us, to hold hands in such a fashion. We had been doing it for years and both enjoyed the clasp.

Way down at the foot of the bed was Luke. I could not see clearly, but it seemed like there were a lot of tears of joy in people's eyes.

Finally I spoke. "Where am I and what am I doing here?" After I thought for a few seconds, I was able to figure out I was in Follansville General Hospital.

Father Matthew spoke. "Welcome back to the world, Jake. I knew you were going to make it, because I used my very special container of holy chrism to anoint you," Father joked.

I was drowsy and I had a headache but was able to respond with what I hoped were statements that made sense.

"Okay. I am in the hospital. When did I get here? What happened? And how long have I been out?"

Dr. Capo responded that I had been in a coma for about five days. He asked, "Jake, do you have any idea what happened?"

"Yes," I replied. "I was crossing the street to go to Bessie's and a car came too close and brushed me. I got up, dusted myself off, and went to Bessie's, assuring everyone I was fine."

Dr. Capo responded, "That's what you think happened, Jake. You did not get up and dust yourself off and go on your way. The guy that hit you sent you flying. You obviously hit your head and were knocked unconscious. Fortunately a guy heading for the mill saw the accident and was able to get a description of the car and some of the license number. Sheriff Drago's office put out an APB and they had the guy in custody within an hour. His blood-alcohol level was way above the legal limit and he had drugs in his system as well. As far as I know, he is still in the county jail."

While my discussion with Dr. Capo was going on, the parade of visitors began. They had all been in the waiting room, and when Luke went out and told them I had become conscious a cheer sounded.

Dr. Capo continued, "The waiting room has been filled with friends who have been in and out for days wondering about your well-being, Jake."

The first to enter was Bessie. She was crying and ran up and gently hugged me. "Jake," she said, "you're awake. I am so happy." She looked at Dr. Capo and said, "He is going to be all right, isn't he, doctor?"

Dr. Capo replied, "He is under the care of some of the best specialists in the area, headed by Dr. Peter Shepard. He and his team are the best around."

The visitors continued. Moose, Louie, Mac, and Butch came in next. I extended a wave to all of them, and thanked them for their concern, and assured them I was going to be fine.

Timmy Bradlee was home from college, and he came by multiple times, and was glad that he made it while I was awake. I asked him if he made a decision on college, recalling our conversation.

"Jake," he replied, "we had that conversation a year ago. I decided to go Division 1, and was fortunate to get a scholarship to Duke University. I am now a Blue Devil instead of a Blue Rider. I'm on the football team and am enrolled in the pre-med program. I remembered what you told me, Jake – a good education is the most important thing, just in case I do not get that big pro contract."

I smiled at Timmy and gave him a thumb up as I thought, good old Mike Kelly, and responded; "Now you're talking."

John and Ann went out to bring in the grandchildren. I gave hugs to James, Lucy, Rosie, Grace, and Jack, and assured them that Pap was going to be fine.

Next Ken Howell and Terry Day arrived. I spoke to them and asked if they had a racing form in the waiting room and if they were handicapping the day's card. Ken gave me a grin and a thumb up, while Terry looked at Ken and said, "He's all right. He's already thinking about the track."

Father Matthew was preparing to leave, but I interrupted his exit. "Father," I asked, "our discussions regarding Kathleen, was that not recently?"

He replied, "No, Jake. We had that conversation during the year of Kathleen's passing."

Now I was really confused. I looked at Dr. Capo and Dr. Shepard who had entered the room and asked, "What has been going on?"

Dr. Shepard told me that after the accident and me being knocked unconscious I went into a coma. While in this coma I was subjected to, in layman's terms, a medical problem referred to as Mind Recall Syndrome.

"You thought you were fine, Jake, but while in the coma you were reliving different years of your life. You were recalling sad times, and when you did you frowned and even cried. I would guess you were thinking about Kathleen and all the sad memories you had while she was going through her last months. Sometimes you would smile, and who knows who you were recalling, but my guess is you and Luke was probably involved in something."

Dr. Shepard continued, "There were times when you were very restless, even having a shortness of breath, as if you were fighting or doing some physical activity. When that happened, the heart monitor and your blood pressure skyrocketed. The nurses responded quickly with medication to get you through the crisis."

I just stared at Dr. Shepard and everyone else in the room. "So the bottom line is I was dreaming all of the different times in my life and there was no rhyme or reason to when they occurred; it could have been something that happened years ago or it could have been something that I had done a week ago?"

Dr. Shepard responded, "That's right, Jake. In your mind you felt like you were living your life, but instead you were dreaming."

I was still holding Jane's hand. Whenever I had physical problems in the past, Jane was always there for me, and here she was at my side again. She is a wonderful lady, and I am grateful to her for all she has done. She will always have a special place in my heart. I gave her hand a squeeze, saying to her, "You always told me I was a dreamer. I guess in this case you are right."

Jane smiled as a tear appeared in her beautiful blue eyes. She put her other hand on top of mine. "It's okay, Jake, you can dream all you want. I am glad you are alive and hopefully going to be well," she said as she looked over to Dr. Shepard. He nodded as if to say, things are going to be fine.

There were smiles on everyone's faces. They all seemed relieved that I had come out of the coma and was on the road to recovery. I spoke to everyone and expressed my appreciation for all their concern. I thanked Dr. Capo and Dr. Shepard for the treatment they and their staff provided me.

The doctors left the room. I asked John and Ann to bring the grandchildren back into the room. Jim, Theresa, Andrew, Mary, David, and Kathryn also remained in the room at my request. Jane thought she should leave, but I would not let go of her hand and insisted that she stay. Once they were all assembled I looked at them.

"We are all family. We must love and respect each other to the highest degree. We must never let any issue divide us. Being a loving and caring family is the most important function in the world. God has allowed me more time to be with all of you, and I hope to take full advantage of this gift any way I can. I love all of you."

"You know," I said, smiling, "people ask me how I am doing, and I reply 'Always living the dream,' but in this case, I guess it was a dream I was living."